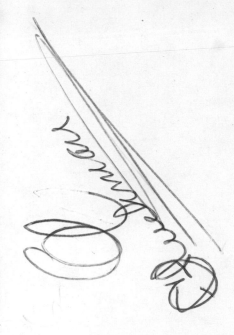

Available in Norton Paperback Fiction

KATERINA

Katerina

Aharon Appelfeld

TRANSLATED FROM THE HEBREW
BY JEFFREY M. GREEN

W. W. Norton & Company
New York • London

Copyright © 1992 by Aharon Appelfeld

Published by arrangement With Random House, Inc.
This work was originally published in Hebrew by Keter Publishing House,
Jerusalem, in 1989. Copyright © 1989 by Aharon Appelfeld and Keter
Publishing House, Jerusalem, Ltd. P.O. Box 7145, Jerusalem, Israel.

First published as a Norton paperback 1994

Printed in the United States of America

The text of this book is set in Galliard

Library of Congress Cataloging-in-Publication Data

Appelfeld, Aron
[Katerinah. English]
Katerina / Aharon Appelfeld : translated from the Hebrew by Jeffrey M. Green
p.   cm.
Previously published: New York : Random House, c1992.
ISBN 0-393-31110-4

1. Antisemitism - Fiction.   2. Poland - History - 1918-1945 - Fiction.
I. Title
[PJ5054.A755K3613   1994]
892.4 ' 36—dc20   93-1520
CIP

W. W. Norton & Company, Inc., 500 Fifth Avenue, New York, N.Y. 10110
W. W. Norton & Company Ltd, 10 Coptic Street, London WC1A 1PU

1 2 3 4 5 6 7 8 9 0

KATERINA

1

MY NAME IS KATERINA, and I will soon be eighty years old. After Easter I returned to my native village and to my father's farm, small and dilapidated, with no building left intact except this hut where I'm living. But it has one single window, open wide, and it allows in the breadth of the world. My eyes, in truth, have grown weaker, but the desire to see still throbs within them. At noon, when the light is most powerful, open space expands before me as far as the banks of the Prut, whose water is blue this season, vibrant with splendor.

I left this place behind more than sixty years ago—to be precise, sixty-three years ago—but it hasn't changed much. The vegetation, that green eternity which envelops these hills, stands tall. If my eyes do not deceive me, it's even greener. A few trees from my distant childhood still stand straight and sprout leaves, not to mention that enchanting, wavelike movement of these hills. Everything is in its place, except for the people. They've all left and gone away.

In the early morning hours, I remove the heavy veils that

obscure the many years and examine them, with silent observation, face to face, as they say in Scripture.

The summer nights in this season are long and splendid, and not only are the oaks reflected in the lake, but the simple reeds also draw vigor from that clear water. I always loved that modest lake, but I especially loved it during the brilliant summer nights, when the line between heaven and earth is erased and the whole cosmos is suffused with heavenly light. The years in a foreign land distanced me from these marvels, and they were obliterated from my memory, but not, apparently, from my heart. Now I know that light is what drew me back. Such purity, oh Lord! Sometimes I wish to stretch out my hand and touch the breezes that meet me on my way, because in this season they are soft as silk.

It's hard to sleep on these brilliant summer nights. Sometimes it seems to me that it's a sin to sleep in this brilliance. I understand now what it says in the Holy Scriptures: "He who stretches out the heaven like a thin curtain." The word *curtain* always sounded strange and distant. Now I can see the thin curtain.

Walking is very hard for me. Without the broad window, which is open wide, without it taking me out and bringing me in, I would be locked up here like in prison, but this opening, by its grace, brings me out easily, and I wander over the meadows as in my youth. Late at night, when the light dims on the horizon, I return to my cage, my hunger sated and my thirst slaked, and I shut my eyes. When I close my eyes I encounter other faces, faces I haven't seen before.

On Sundays I pull myself together and go down to the chapel. The distance from my hut to the chapel isn't great, a quarter of an hour's walk. In my youth I used to cover the distance in a single bound. Then all my life was a single puff of breeze, but today, though every step is painful, that walk is still very important to me. These stones awaken my memory, especially the memory from before memory, and I see not only my departed mother but everyone who ever passed over these paths, knelt, wept, and prayed. For some reason it now seems that they all used to wear fur coats. Maybe because of a nameless peasant, who came here secretly, prayed, and afterward took his life with his own hand. His shouts pierced my temples.

The chapel building is old and rickety yet lovely in its simplicity. The wooden buttresses that my father installed still protect it. My father wasn't scrupulous about keeping our religion, but he saw it as his duty not to neglect this small sanctuary. I remember, as though in a twilight, the beams he carried on his shoulders, thick staves, and the way he pounded them into the earth with a huge wooden mallet. My father seemed like a giant to me then, and his work was the work of giants. Those beams, though they've rotted, are still rooted in their place. Inanimate objects live a long life; only man is snatched away untimely.

Whoever thought I would come back here? I had erased this first bosom from my memory like an animal, but a person's memory is stronger than he is. What the will doesn't do is done by necessity, and necessity ultimately becomes will. I'm not sorry I returned. Apparently, it was ordained.

I sit on the low bench in the chapel for an hour or two. The silence here is massive, perhaps because of the valley that surrounds the place. As a girl I used to run after cows and goats on these trails. How blind and marvelous my life was then. I was like one of the animals I drove, strong like them and just as mute. Of those years no outward trace remains, just me, the years crammed into me, and my old age. Old age brings a person closer to himself and to the dead. The beloved dead bring us close to God.

In this valley I heard a voice from on high for the first time—actually, it was in the lowest slopes of this valley, where it opens up and flows into a broad plain. I remember the voice with great clarity. I was seven, and suddenly I heard a voice, not my mother's or father's, and the voice said to me, "Don't be afraid, my daughter. You shall find the lost cow." It was an assured voice, and so calm that it instantly removed the fear from my heart. I sat frozen and watched. The darkness grew thicker. There was no sound, and suddenly the cow emerged from the darkness and came up to me. Ever since then, when I hear the word *salvation*, I see that brown cow I had lost and who came back to me. That voice addressed me only once, never again. I never told anyone about it. I kept that secret hidden in my heart, and I rejoiced in it. In those years I was afraid of every shadow. In truth, I was prey to fear for many years and only free of it when I reached an advanced age. If I had prayed, prayer would have taught me not to be afraid. But my fate decreed otherwise, if I may say. The lesson came to me many years too late, immersed in many bitter experiences.

In my youth, I had no desire either for prayer or for the Holy Scriptures. The words of prayers that I intoned were not my own. I went to church because my mother forced me. At the age of twelve, I had visions of obscenities in the middle of prayers, which greatly darkened my spirit. Every Sunday I used to pretend to be sick, and as much as my mother hit me, nothing did any good. I was as afraid of church as I was of the village doctor.

Nevertheless, thank God, I didn't cut myself off from the wellsprings of faith. There were moments in my life when I forgot myself, when I sank into filth, when I lost the image of God, but even then I often would fall to my knees and pray. Remember, God, those few moments, because my sins were many, and only Thou, with Thy great mercy, know the soul of Thy handmaiden.

Now, as the proverb says, the water has flowed back into the river, the circle is closed, and I have returned here. The days are full and splendid, and I wander at great length. As long as the window is open and my eyes are awake, loneliness doesn't grieve my soul. Too bad the dead are forbidden to speak. They have something to say, I'm sure.

Once a week blind Chamilio brings me supplies from the village. My needs are now very few—three or four cups of tea, bread, and farmer's cheese. There's plenty of fruit here. I have already tasted the cherries, pure wine.

Chamilio isn't young any longer, but his blind gait is steady. He gropes with his thick staff, and his staff never betrays him. When he bends over, I discover a strong line in his back. They told me that when he was young, the women clung to him. No wonder; he was handsome. Now, see what the years have done to him. First he became deaf and then he went blind and now there are only remnants of him. When he approaches my hut with the bundle on his shoulders, he seems heavy and submissive for some reason, but that's only an illusion.

When I left the village he had just been born, but I heard

a lot about him, not always favorable gossip. After years of bachelorhood and wild living, he had married. The bride was pretty and rich and she brought a considerable dowry, but she wasn't faithful. They said that was his punishment because he had deceived so many women, but she too was punished for her infidelities: A swarm of hornets attacked her in the middle of a field and killed her. For once it seemed as though reward and punishment had been meted out in this world, but who am I to judge about that mysterious balance.

Every Thursday, Chamilio comes and brings me my food. God knows how he finds his way. To my mind he's an otherworldly creature. Without him I would be lying in the dust.

"Thank you, Chamilio," I say loudly. I doubt whether he can hear me. In any case, he makes a small grimace as though driving away a thought. When I put something in his big palm, he bangs on the floor with his thick staff, muttering something, then leaves. His clothes give off the smell of grass and water. He apparently spends most of the day outdoors.

"How are you?" I ask him, and immediately see the stupidity of my question. He does his work quietly and steadily. First he arranges the supplies in the pantry, and then he brings in chopped wood and lays it near the stove, everything done quietly and diligently. For about an hour he works. In that hour he fills my hut with the aromas of the fields, a perfume lingering with me all week long.

I love to sit and follow him with my gaze as he walks away, a slow departure that sometimes lasts a full hour. First he goes down to the chapel, prostrates himself at the threshold, and prays. Sometimes it seems to me that I can hear his silence. Suddenly, he rouses himself, without fuss, as though turning his back, rises, and walks down to the lake. Near the lake, his strides halt and his feet stop.

Sometimes it seems to me that he tarries in order to inhale the smell of the water. In this season the lake water has a fragrance. He does indeed approach the edge of the lake, bends over, but doesn't linger, and immediately slips down the path and is swallowed among the trees.

When he disappears among the trees, he appears before my eyes again with a different kind of clarity, sturdy and handsome, and I begin to miss him. The darkness makes me forget him all at once, and only on Thursday morning does his warm odor enter my nostrils, and I remember him, and a tremor of expectation runs down my back.

On most days I sit in my armchair, a wooden armchair upholstered with thick cushions. The years have not harmed it; it still takes pity on a person's bones. Here my mother used to sit on Sundays, her eyes shut, all the week's weariness stamped on her face, her hair thin and gray. Now I am forty years older than she was. The tables have turned—the mother is young and the daughter is aged, and that, it seems, is how things will remain forever. When the dead are reborn, she will certainly be astonished: Is this my daughter, Katerina? Nevertheless, when I pray for my life I also pray to her. I'm certain that our mothers protect us, that without them and their virtues, the wicked would long since have done away with us.

Most of the day I sit and gaze out. Before my eyes the lake flickers in its brilliant hues. In this season its light is dazzling. Once, abundant life rustled here, and now there is only silence. When I listen to the silence, distant sights rise up from the meadows and fill my eyes. Yesterday, I had a very clear vision. I was three and sitting in the pasture and our shepherd dog, Zimbi, was licking my fingers. Father was sitting under a tree, slowly getting drunk from a bottle of vodka, happy and content. Father, I call out for some reason. He's so immersed in his drinking, he doesn't answer. I sob and cry, but my sobbing doesn't move him from his place. Mother bursts out of the house like a storm wind, and I immediately fall silent.

My mother, of blessed memory, was an unfortunate woman and we all dreaded her, even my sturdy father. Not even the cows dared defy her. I remember how, with her bare hands, she once subdued a crazed cow. Her hands, God forgive me, scar my body till today. She would beat me for everything, serious or trifling, with fury and without mercy. Easter was the only time she wouldn't beat me. At Easter her face would change, and a silent awe came into her eyes, like a fast-flowing river whose waters grow placid. At Easter her face would radiate light throughout the house: a kind of piety that didn't belong to this place.

I would spend Easter on a ledge, next to Zimbi. I treasure Zimbi's memory with pleasant warmth. He was a sturdy dog. He liked people and especially children. If there is any warmth in my body, it is the warmth I absorbed from him. His odor still clings to my nostrils. When I left the house he whimpered bitterly, as though he knew I wouldn't come back to see him. For me, he still lives, especially his barks, restrained barks, that always sounded to me like friendly greetings. My soul cleaved to his, if I may say. Since my return, I sometimes hear his whimpers, and I miss his round, soft body, his silky fur, and the smell of the river that clung to his paws.

My mother also loved Zimbi. But her love was different, hemmed in, without contact. But that mute creature apparently sensed that this unfortunate woman had a feeling for him, and he would jump toward her with affection. He was deathly frightened of my father. Sometimes I sense that I am tied to my late mother through Zimbi's body. Our love for Zimbi bound our souls together with a hidden force. Only God knows the secrets of the heart, and only God knows what joins us together in life and death.

Right after Easter, the light in her face went out and anger would cloud it again. When I was still little, I heard people say: "She's very unfortunate. She must be pitied. Her offspring died as infants." I was certain that the angel of death would not pass over me. Every night I would pray for my life. And, wonder of wonders, the prayers worked, and my life has been prolonged beyond man's allotted span.

My mother died very young. Her face is as clear to me as on the day she left us. I especially see the angry swing of her long arms. Even today, many years later, I remember her with fear and trembling, as the Scriptures say. Every time I think about her, she comes toward me with rage. Why, Mother, I ask, are you angry at me? I have already been punished for my sins, and I shall be whipped for my transgressions in the world of truth. But my mother is obstinate. She is very young, and she will stay young for all eternity. If she had lived as long as I, her blood would have been calmer. At my age, no one gets angry any longer.

Sometimes it seems to me that she bears us all a grudge because we buried her in the ice. The cemetery was barren

and white, and the two gravediggers carved out her plot
with axes. The people stood at a distance from the pit and
shivered. The priest fumed at the gravediggers for their
laziness, for not preparing the trench in time. The priest's
face was gray, and he urged the gravediggers on with mum-
bled words that sounded like curses.

Afterward, in the dark already, the prayers dropped like
hail. I wrapped my head in a kerchief to avoid seeing the
coffin lowered into the pit on ropes, but the cold penetrated
to my bones anyway, and I feel it to this very day.

Right after Mother's death, Father sank into heavy drunkenness. He neglected the house and farm, sold the embroidered cloths and even my mother's dowry chest. Now I
became afraid of him, as though he were a stranger. He
would return home late at night and immediately collapse
onto his bed like a corpse. He slept most of the day, stirring
only toward evening, and without delay, he would head for
the tavern.

In the spring he didn't go out to the field. He ignored
me as though I didn't exist. Sometimes he would brandish
his fist at me and slap my face, distractedly, the way one
swats a fly. My mother's death freed him to drink as he
wanted. Sometimes he would come home in a gay mood,
like a wild young man.

One night he approached me, may God forgive me, and
spoke to me in a voice that wasn't his: "Why not sleep with
Daddy? The house is cold." His eyes were glassy, and a kind
of wanton redness glowed in them. He had never spoken
to me in a voice like that. "It's good to sleep with Daddy,"
he said to me again in the voice that wasn't his. I felt in my
heart that this was sinful, but I didn't know for sure. I

crawled under the table like a dog and didn't utter a word. Father crouched on his knees and said, "Why are you running away from me? It's your daddy, not a stranger." Then he put his two huge hands on my shoulders, pulled me to him, and kissed me. He then got to his feet, made a dismissive gesture, and sank onto his bed, asleep. After that, he didn't look at me again.

2

A FEW MONTHS AFTER my mother's death, Father brought a new wife home. She was a tall, broad woman who never spoke a word. The mountain from which she came was embodied in her face: a cramped face, like a workhorse's. Father used to talk to her in a loud voice, as though to someone deaf.

"What are you doing?" she would ask me in a frightening tone.

"I?" I recoiled in my great fear.

"You've got to work," she said. "You can't sit idle."

I used to spend most of the day outdoors. Even then I knew that this life would pass away and that another life, different and distant from here, would emerge from it. Every night I used to see my mother in a dream, and she, as always, was busy with housework, debts, and sick cattle. "Mother!" I wanted to have her near me, but she, as in life, was angry at everyone. I told her that Father had brought home a new wife. She seemed to grasp the fact, but ignored it.

In the autumn, I left the house. "Where to?" asked my father.

"To work."

"Be careful, and don't step off the straight and narrow path," he called, and without adding a word, he disappeared from my sight. My father was a powerful man; he didn't dare strike my mother, but I heard that he used to beat his second wife fiercely. They told me that he changed in the final years of his life and started going to church on Sundays.

I can hear my mother's presence simmering and hissing, but I see my father before me as though he has refused to leave this world. In the summer many years ago, my father once stood leaning on a long pitchfork and smacked his lips to the cows, as if he were blowing kisses to slutty girls. The cows looked at him and smiled, which tickled his fancy, and he kept on smacking his lips. A strange kind of intimacy heated up between him and the cows. That summer, when I was in the third grade, on my way to school I suddenly heard my father's voice: "Where is she going?"

"To school," Mother answered without raising her head.

"What good does it do her? They don't learn anything."

"You're not a priest. The priest ordered us to send the girls to school."

"I say no." A spirit of foolishness arose within him.

But my mother wasn't alarmed, and she told him, "There is a God in heaven and He is king and He is the father, and we are ordered to heed Him, not you."

Mother was a strong and brave woman. I saw her courage once in the winter, when she fought with a horse thief and made him run for his life. But for some reason she did not bequeath that courage to me. I was afraid of every shadow and listened for every sound; at night, even the crickets would alarm me.

This isolated place gave me no joy, but my first memories are still crystal clear: the rains, for example, the furious rains, or the harrowing rains, as they call them here. For my part, I loved the swift rains of the summer and the mist that used to rise from the meadows after a shower.

I never see my father and my mother together. As if they had never been together. Each of them had a special connection with animals. My mother took care of them devotedly but coldly; a healthy cow didn't count for her. My father, in contrast, had a provocative relation with them, as if they were women to be seduced.

My mother was contemptuous of him for that behavior. After my mother's death, I occasionally used to visit the chapel. She seemed to be lying on the large icon and praying together with the Holy Mother. I used to sit and watch the women praying, forlorn women. Sometimes they would hand me a piece of cake and bless me. There, among the smoky candles, the mildew, and the offerings I learned to observe people.

My father and his new wife did not, apparently, have a happy life. My mother's spirit hovered in every corner. The new wife, the stranger, tried in vain to dislodge her from her domain. More than once I heard her grumble, "I can't manage to do anything. In my house everybody was pleased with me, and here everything goes wrong." Father, of course, didn't accept these excuses, and every time bread burned in the oven or the food spoiled, he would hit her. She used to screech and threaten to run home. Years later, I heard that she dished out her fair share too, and when my father got sick, she treated him shabbily. There were rumors that she poisoned him. Who knows? She too is in the world of truth. If she sinned, she'll pay her due. All accounts are settled in the end.

Something else, no small matter, used to be whispered about the house: my father's bastards. Mother, of course, never forgave him, and she would often remind him of his sin. Each time she mentioned it, a peculiar smile would spread over his face, as if it weren't a sin anymore but some trivial lapse. He had two bastards, from the same woman —a notorious harlot. In my childhood, I had seen them with my own eyes: sturdy young men, sitting on a narrow wagon and driving two skinny horses. Their way of perching on the narrow wagon struck me as funny. At a second glance, I discovered they looked like my father. "Mine die and the bastards live and thrive," I heard my mother say more than once, gritting her teeth.

I left home with neither pain nor remorse, taking the back road everyone calls the Jewish road. Here, in the spring, but also in the winter, thin Jews used to gather, like grasshoppers, and sell their wares. They were one of the frightening wonders of my childhood. With their appearance, their way of sitting and bargaining, they weren't like creatures of this world but like dark spirits scuttling about on spindly legs. "Don't go there." I heard my mother's voice more than once. That warning just increased my curiosity, and every time they appeared, I would be there. They used to place their suitcases on the ground and spread out their wares in front of everyone. They had many ways of displaying: on ropes they would stretch from tree to tree, on improvised stands, on twigs, or simply on the ground. Those little, wrinkled suitcases proved to be full of treasures: colorful shirts, stockings, high-heeled shoes, and embroidered underwear—mostly women's clothing and women's finery. The women would swoop down on the garments and snatch whatever they could. I loved the city smells, cloaked in embroidered nightshirts.

If you ignored their frightening presence, the sight was diverting. I envied the women who used to bargain and buy new things, which would be wrapped in papers and cardboard. I didn't have a penny. Once I asked my mother for a coin to buy a candy, and she scolded me, saying: "Don't go there. The Jews will cheat you." For hours I used to sit there. The peddlers were short and lively, and sometimes it seemed that they didn't walk on human legs but rather on birds' legs, so they could hop. Occasionally, a few peasants would appear abruptly and drive them away with whips. Once, in their flight, they left behind a pair of colorful stockings. When I showed them to my mother, she said, "Don't wear them now. Save them for the holy days."

Mostly, they would sell until evening. Then they would pack up the remainder of their wares and disappear. Once a Jew stood in our courtyard and offered us his wares. He was tall and thin, fringed with a black beard, and his neck was slender and long. Such a bare neck I had never seen in my life.

Afterward, I got used to them, and sometimes I would steal a piece of cloth or a little packet of candy. I particularly remember those thefts. There was a kind of victory over fear in them and a repressed joy, because you were allowed to steal from them—or as my mother used to say, theft from a thief is permitted.

Once my cousin Maria called to me, "The ghosts have arrived, and you're here?"

"What ghosts are you talking about?"

"The ghosts with the suitcases."

"You frightened me, Maria."

"No need to be frightened," she said coldly. "If you get used to them, you can get just what you need out of them."

My cousin Maria was seven years older. She had worked for the Jews, and she knew them at close hand. She, too, like all of us, despised them, but she already knew that they weren't openly harmful, that they didn't poison you. She had dresses and underwear she had received from them. Once she brought an embroidered slip and gave it to me as a present.

My cousin Maria, may she rest in peace, was, God forgive her, as cold as ice. She didn't know the meaning of fear. More than once I saw her stick a pig. She stabbed it without repugnance, and when the poor thing squealed, the expression on her face didn't change. I once heard her cursing like a man. In the spring, I remember, she went up to one of the booths, chose a pretty shirt, and asked its price. The Jew named a sum.

"I don't have any money today," she said. "Next time I'll pay you."

"I won't sell it to you," said the Jew.

"What do you mean, you won't sell?" She spoke to him softly and firmly. "You'll be sorry."

"I haven't wronged anyone." He raised his voice.

"If you don't give it to me, my brother will slaughter you in the field," she hissed.

"I'm not afraid," the Jew shouted.

"Too bad to die for a shirt," she whispered, running away with it. The Jew was about to run after her, and he did take a couple of steps, but he didn't go far. That very night Maria explained to me, "The Jews, unlike us, are afraid of death. That fear is their undoing. That's their weakness. We'll jump off a bridge, but they won't. That's the difference, understand?" Maria, God forgive her, was a brazen woman. I myself was afraid of her.

In the village, the Jews used to appear at any time and in places you wouldn't have expected them, near the lake or behind the chapel. The way they dressed made them very conspicuous. People would beat them or run after them, but, like the crows, they used to return, in every season of the year.

"Why are they like that?" I once asked my mother.

"Don't you know? They killed Jesus."

"They?"

"They."

I didn't ask any more. I was afraid to ask. They filled my dreams and blackened many nights. They always had the same look: thin, swarthy, hopping on birds' legs, and suddenly rising up. Once, I remember, a Jew crossed my path in the middle of the field. He handed me a piece of candy, but so great was my fear that I took to my heels as though fleeing a ghost.

3

FOR TWO DAYS I trampled along. Fall was everywhere, rain and thick fog, but more bitter than anything was my father's indifferent gaze. He abandoned me the way you abandon a sick animal that you don't want put down right away. I wasn't afraid of dogs. I was used to dogs. Every time a dog crossed my path, I stood still and made friends with it, for I understand the language of dogs. Judging by the way they bark, I know whether they're content or angry. Wild dogs are mute. It's hard to admit it, but we're closer to animals than to humans. How many friends does a person acquire in his lifetime?

Between one rainstorm and another I would pick an apple or a pear, sit down, and try to cling to my mother's memory. With no living soul nearby, a person draws close to the dead. My mother was a bitter woman in her lifetime, and in death her bitterness increased. More than once I asked mercy for her. Even in the world of truth she's consumed by bitterness. Doesn't death release us from our worldly accounts? Is everything we did, all the stupidity and filth,

eternally bound to us? At night, I slept on a threshing floor
or in an abandoned shed. From my earliest childhood I was
accustomed to damp. Anyone who was born in a village
knows that life is no party. I didn't cry, and I didn't blame
anyone, but I lingered in the chapels and prayed. In the
low, miserable chapels I learned how to pray. It's hard to
overcome pride and bend the knee, but when a person leaves
his home and he has no other home in the world, his knees
bend by themselves. In those poor chapels one learns how
to approach one's fellow man with a humble heart. Near
those houses of worship, people handed me a slice of cake,
a piece of cheese. I even got a coin from one peasant. Not
every time. I occasionally saw a peasant woman come out
of the chapel and fall upon her animal, beating it savagely,
as if it weren't a dumb beast but a notorious criminal.

I got to Strassov one night, a town consisting of a street
and a busy railroad station. Maria had told me a lot about
the town, but the sight of it wasn't the way I had imagined
it. The people poured out and crowded together near the
exit, trains came and went, and tall, hearty men stood on
the platforms and loaded sacks of grain.

"Don't let them nuzzle you," Maria had warned me.

Later, the station emptied out, the trains stopped running,
the buffet was locked, and beggars and drunks popped out
of the dark corners.

"Who are you?" one of the drunks asked me.

I was startled, and my mouth was dumb.

"From what village?" he kept asking.

I told him.

"Come with us; soon we'll make some coffee."

That's how I got to know the night world of the railroad station. I was sixteen years old. They all called me the baby girl. That wasn't an indulgent term there. If a person doesn't give his due, he's thrown out even from that cold, dark corner.

The next day I started washing dishes in the restaurant. Anyone born in a village is used to abuse. My mother beat me and my father didn't spare my body, either. The restaurant owner was no better than they. In the evening, before paying me, he would feel my breasts. At night, many hands pawed me. It was cold in the dark, and the poor people's clothing gave off a strong smell of damp. That foul smell came to cling to my clothes, too. "*The body's not holy, nothing will happen to you*," said one of the drunks, reaching out and feeling my crotch.

The autumn turned out to be cold in the city. If I had had a room, I would have run away. A person without a room is like a stray dog. Everyone molests him. Having no choice, I used to sit, give them my things, and take theirs. I gave them the pennies that I earned, and they gave me a drink and a cup of coffee. I knew that drink deadens fear. My mother didn't drink vodka outside the house, but during the dark winter days she used to sit alone and get drunk. When she got drunk, a hint of her youth would return to her face. She used to tell me about her native village, about the festivals and celebrations. I liked those rare hours very much, but the next day she would get up bitter and furious, casting her dread upon me.

In the Strassov railway station I learned how to swallow a whole drink in one gulp. After two or three drinks, you no longer feel fear or pain; you even enjoy the snuggling. In fact, nothing bothers you anymore; you lean your head against the wall, close your eyes, and sing.

One night, while I was still curled up with the drunks, my mother appeared to me, full of dread and anger.

"How did you get here?" I asked stupidly.

"You're asking me?" she answered in anger.

I wanted to bend my knees and ask her pardon, but she disappeared, just as in her lifetime, furiously and with the rush of a person who doesn't consider other people's opinions. The next day I told one of the drunken women about the dream. She dismissed it with a wave of her hand and said, "Don't listen to her. My mother used to torment me in dreams, too. I don't believe in anyone, not even the dead. Everybody tries to take advantage of you. I wouldn't go back to the village for anything. My body's worthless in my eyes. If anyone wants to sleep with me, I let him. It's warmer for both of us."

So the days passed with no end in sight. The restaurant, for some reason, fired me. Now I didn't have a penny. I would steal whatever came to hand. I was caught more than once, and more than once they beat me, but I didn't cry and I didn't beg for mercy. I just gritted my teeth.

The promises the boys made to me were untrue. All that autumn they fondled my flesh, but when the cold got more bitter, they cleared out and left me alone with the sick and the old. Old people know when their end is near, and they curl up in a corner and wait for it silently. They say that freezing to death isn't painful, but I have seen for myself how people writhe with the sting of cold and moan in agony. Who listens to them in a busy railroad station? Everyone goes his own way. That winter I cursed my father for not giving me a penny to live on.

But no darkness is absolute, though it sometimes seems so. While I was standing, abandoned in the busy railroad station, a short woman approached me and asked me simply, "Do you want to work for me?" I don't know what an angel of God looks like, but that woman's voice sounded to me like a voice from on high. From nearby, I could see that her face, wrapped in a kerchief, wasn't soft. A kind of sternness was congealed in her eyes. I don't like short people. They always instill a kind of restlessness and a guilt in me. "If someone gives you shelter in the cold, you have to love him," I said to myself, and followed her.

"Where do you come from?" she asked.

I told her.

"And have you ever seen Jews?"

"Occasionally." I smiled.

"I'm Jewish. Are you afraid?"

"No."

"But first of all you must have a bath." It had been months since my body had seen water. My clothes were sodden with the odor of damp, vodka, and tobacco; a person gets so accustomed to filth that he no longer notices it. Now, as I stood naked, fear coursed through my entire body and made me shudder. From every side Jews came up and stood next to me, and they were all in the same image: a thin man with a drawn sword in his hand. I fell to my knees and crossed myself. My sins had reached the high heavens, and now I was about to pay.

That night I remembered the Jews who used to wander through our village, skipping among the trees and courtyards or standing next to their improvised stands, living ghosts, talking ghosts, and I remembered the peasants who would appear and crack their whips at them. Now, for some reason, it seemed that they were lighter, skipping over trenches and fences; their earthly weight seemed to have been removed. "You can't vanquish them,"—I heard Maria's laugh. "A ghost's body feels no pain." The peasants kept on whipping, and Maria's laughter, her hearty laughter, was swallowed up in the crack of the blows. I awoke.

4

"I'm with the Jews," I said, and I didn't know what I was saying. I burned my damp and ragged clothes that night. The cast-off clothes from the lady of the house fit me. They were clean, odorless, and for some reason aroused my suspicion that they had belonged to dead Jews. The lady of the house apparently noticed my apprehension, opened the door, and showed me the apartment: three dingy, not very large rooms—a dining room and two bedrooms.

"Have you ever seen Jews before?" she asked again.

"They used to come to the village to sell their wares."

The work was simple but oppressive. My mother and father had taught me to work but not to be meticulous, and here I had to be careful about every single pot. The man of the house, a tall and reserved man, used to sit at the head of the table and, after saying the blessing, didn't utter a word. The Jews' religion, if you don't know, is restrained.

The lady of the house didn't spoil me. With great rigor she taught me what was forbidden and what was permitted. *Kashrut*, that's what they call the separation between milk and meat. For them, strict observance of *kashrut* is connected with a kind of continual concern, as though it weren't a matter of household utensils and food but of feelings. For many years I tried to fathom that concern.

Had it not been winter, I would have fled. Even wretched freedom is freedom, and here were nothing but prohibitions. But when I peeked out of the window, I saw snow piled on all the roofs, the traffic in the streets sparse, no one going in and out of the stores. I didn't have the courage to leap into that frost.

I haven't mentioned the two boys, Abraham and Meir. The elder was seven and the younger, six. Two pinkish, merry creatures, like two old clowns, who would suddenly fall silent, fixing you with their big eyes, as though you were a creature from another world.

The youngsters studied from early morning till late in the evening. That's not the way to teach children; that's how you train priests and monks. Among us, we scarcely studied for four hours. With them they stick a book in a baby's hand before he opens his eyes; is it any wonder that their faces are puffy and pinkish? Among us, a child swims in the river, goes fishing, and catches a colt on the run. My entire being recoiled at the sight of those youngsters being led to their prison early each morning. At that time, I hated the Jews. There's nothing easier than to hate the Jews.

I used to spend Sundays with my own kind in the tavern. Most of them also worked for the Jews—some in their yards, some in their stores. Our impressions were identical. Our youth, the joy we took in life, made us hold the Jews in contempt—their height, their dress, their food, their language, the way they dressed and mated. Not a detail escaped our eyes. What we didn't know, our imagination filled in, and imagination, after two or three drinks, flourished.

We vied with each other in telling jokes. We used to sing and curse the children of Satan, amongst whom everything is accounts, money, investment, and interest. Everything done in measure—eating, drinking, and copulation. For hours on end we would bawl:

> *The Jews have plenty of banknotes,*
> *But they only pay pennies to you.*
> *They take a bath on Thursday,*
> *And on Friday night they screw.*

In the spring I knew I was pregnant. I was seventeen. I knew that pregnant girls get fired on the spot, so I didn't say a word to the lady of the house. I made an effort to do the work attentively, not to cheat and not to steal, but as for the boy who had done what he did to me—I lay in wait for him. He made an odd movement with his head and said, "You should go back to the village. In the village no one pays attention to that."

"We're not going to marry?"

"I don't have a penny."

"And what about the child?"

"Leave him in a convent. That's what everybody does."

I knew that words would do no good. Shouting would only make him angrier, but still, how could I not say anything? So, stupidly, I asked, "What about your promises?"

"What promises are you talking about?" he said, and his face blushed with anger. My mouth shut and I turned away.

Now I don't remember his height, whether he was tall

or short, and his face has been completely erased from my memory, but the baby girl, flesh of my flesh, I cannot forget her. It is as though I hadn't abandoned her, as though she had grown up with me. Years ago I had a dream, and in my dream I led her to the altar. The girl was as lovely as an angel, and I called her Angela. Who knows, perhaps she still walks in the land of the living.

Again, I've put the cart before the horse. In my fifth month, I revealed my secret to the lady of the house. I was sure she would fire me on the spot. But to my surprise, she didn't. I remained in the house and kept working. The work wasn't easy, but she didn't rush me and she didn't reproach me with my disgrace. Without noticing it, I got used to the odors of the house, to the strange separation between milk and meat, to the thin darkness that reigned from morning to evening.

In my ninth month of pregnancy I traveled to Moldovitsa, and there, next to the convent, I asked about renting a room with an old peasant woman. The old woman knew why I had come to her right away, and she asked for a high rent. I didn't have any money. I had a stolen piece of gold jewelry, and that's what I offered her.

"How did you get that?"

"I inherited it from my mother."

"Don't disturb your poor mother's rest, and don't tell lies."

"What should I tell you, mother?"

"Tell the truth."

"It's hard to tell it, mother."

The old woman took the jewelry from my hand and asked no more questions.

I could see the convent walls from my window, the steeple with the bells and the meadows that surrounded the convent. I stood beside that window for many hours, and in the evening my head was heavy and dizzy.

"You must pray, my daughter."

"It's hard for me to pray."

"Blindfold yourself with a kerchief. The eyes are the great seducers of sin. Without eyes it's easier to pray." I did as she ordered and tightened the kerchief around my eyes.

The pregnancy went beyond term, and I walked around the walls of the convent day after day, the way the children of Israel marched around Jericho. My desire to enter it, to touch the altar and prostrate myself at its feet, was strong but I didn't dare. When I came back from the meadows, the fear of God would seize me. For a few days I controlled myself, but finally I told the old woman about it.

"What are you afraid of, my daughter?" She spoke to me softly.

"Of God."

"You have nothing to fear. You'll leave the baby in a box, the way they left Moses, and after that the good Lord will do what He thinks best. The nuns are merciful, and they will take care of him. Every month women come here and leave their babies. The babies will be educated in the convent, and they'll become priests and monks."

Every morning the old woman made porridge for me. My body was swollen, and weariness forced me to the couch. I no longer had the strength to approach the convent walls, and I no longer walked far. The old woman urged me to pray every morning. "You mustn't be lazy. A person must get up in the morning and do his duty." Her words of reproach pierced my body like nails. I knew that my sin could not be atoned for.

The birth was hard and painful. The midwife said that she hadn't seen such a difficult birth in years. If someone comes to give birth here, people aren't respectful of her honor. The midwife had no respect for me: "From now on, don't believe men. Do you promise?"

"I promise."

"How do I know you'll keep your promise?"

"I swear."

"People violate oaths easily."

"What shall I do, mother?"

"I'll put a chain on your ankle, and it will always remind you that you mustn't sleep with boys."

"Thank you, mother."

"Don't thank me. Don't sleep with boys, and that will be my reward."

The next day I was about to abandon my baby, but I didn't have the strength to get up. The old woman wasn't happy, but she didn't drive me away. She stood by my bedside and told me about her distant youth, her husband and children. Her husband had departed as a young man, and her daughters hadn't taken the right path. They had been ruined in the city. Now she had nothing in the world but these four walls.

"And where do you work?" she asked suddenly.

"For Jews."

"Is this the Jews'?"

"It's from our kind," I said. "Ours."

In the evening, she softened and tried to console me. The nuns in the convent would raise her and call her Angela.

Sometimes it was good for a person not to have any memory of father or mother. He draws faith straight from the heavens. We were all made in sin. You have suffered enough. From now on the church will take care. In the church everything is clean and quiet. Our lives here pass in turmoil, and there is sublime tranquility. You have nothing to worry about. You're doing the right thing. Without noticing, I had closed my eyes and fallen asleep.

The baby girl nursed without letup and wore me out. If she hadn't worn me out, perhaps I would have stayed longer. For a week I sheltered and nursed her. At the end of the week, my strength failed. I asked the old woman to bring me the basket so I could cushion it on the bottom with my own hands. The old woman helped me quietly. Thus my sinful deed ended. The next day, while darkness was still spread over the meadows, I placed the baby in the basket. The baby was asleep, at rest, and she didn't make a sound. I crossed the fields with long strides, and at the convent gate, I summoned up my courage and left the basket on the stoop.

Sometimes during the long winter nights I see her at a distance, tall and thin, wrapped in many veils of light, as beautiful as the paintings in a church. We have gone a long way, I say to myself, and I sense that soon we shall be face to face, without barriers. My faith in the world to come sometimes floods me like a warm wave.

5

I RETURNED AND SANK INTO my work as though into oblivion. Strange is the life of the Jews. Over the years I learned
to observe them. They are fearfully diligent. After morning
prayers, the master of the house goes out to work in his
store, not a large shop, on the edge of the market, and later
his wife joins him, and they work together without a break
and without having a drink until the evening. I am in the
house, cleaning and straightening up. The house is as full
of books as a convent. My cousin Maria informed me once
that on the eighth day they circumcise the boy babies, so
as to heighten their virility when they mature. One needn't
believe every word that leaves Maria's lips. She mostly ex-
aggerates or makes things up, but she isn't a complete liar.
She, for example, isn't afraid of Jews. She assured me that
no ill would befall me with them.

The trip to Moldovitsa was forgotten. Had it not been
for my dreams at night, life would have gone smoothly for
me then. In dreams, my sins lay spread out before me, the
way only sins can lie open, in all their searing hues. More

than once I heard Angela's voice: "Mommy, Mommy, why did you abandon me?" But in daylight, the slate was wiped clean. I learned to work without talking much. In the village people say that the Jews are chatterboxes, splitting hairs about every little thing to cheat you. They don't know Jews. Speech is only for practical needs. Speech for its own sake doesn't exist with them. There's a kind of compulsion in their industry.

Is theirs a good life? Are they happy? I asked myself more than once. "A person should do his allotted task and ask for no reward," the lady of the house once told me. Still they aspire to greatness. They don't deprive themselves of the pleasures of this world, but there's no avidity in seeking them. The Jews keep taverns, but they themselves don't get drunk.

Not only was I observing them, it appears. They too watched my steps closely. They noticed, for example, that I didn't go out to have a good time on Saturday nights. The lady of the house was content, but she didn't express her approval in so many words. Direct speech isn't common with them.

My loveliest hours were spent with the boys. Boys are boys; though it's true they have an extra dose of cleverness, they're not spirits.

After a few months I gave in to temptation and went back to the tavern. My acquaintances were astounded: "What's the matter with you, Katerina?"

"Nothing at all." I tried to apologize.

Nevertheless, something within me had changed. I had a couple of drinks, but my spirits didn't soar. Everyone around me, the young and the not so young, looked coarse and clumsy to me. I kept on drinking, but I didn't get drunk.

"Where are you working?"

"With the Jews."

"The Jews are having a bad influence on you," a young woman said to me.

"I have no other work."

"You could join me. I'm working in a canteen."

"I'm used to it already."

"You mustn't get used to them."

"Why?"

"I don't know. They have a bad influence. After a year or two a person starts making their gestures. I knew a girl, a good friend, who worked for the Jews. After two years she lost the look of a healthy person. Her face got pale, and her movements had no freedom—a kind of trembling of the jaws. Our life is different. I wouldn't work for them for any amount of money."

I won't hide the truth. At that time I felt a strong attraction toward the master of the house. I don't know what aroused me—his height, his pale face, his prayers in the early morning hours, the coat, or perhaps the footsteps at night. My young body, which had known disgrace and pain, was aroused. In secret, I waited for the night when he would approach my bed.

Apparently, the Jews are very sensitive. Without saying a word, the lady of the house kept me away from the kitchen at mealtimes, and on the Sabbath I wasn't permitted to be in the dining room. The distance didn't blunt my desire. On the contrary, it intensified. In the village I had been drawn to the shepherd, and in the city the boys had lusted for my flesh and devoured it. This time it was a different desire. But what could I do, bite my own flesh? Had I had the courage, I would have gone to the priest and confessed, but I was afraid the priest would reproach me and impose fasts and vows. I didn't then understand that my desires were rooted: Imperceptibly, I had become bound up with the Jews.

My friends at the tavern were right: The Jews have a quiet power to charm. When I first came to their house, it had seemed that they were turned inward and gloomy and that they took little interest in strangers. Sometimes they seemed stooped, as though pervaded by depression. And sometimes arrogance flashed from their eyes and I didn't seem to exist. But after two years of service a change took place. Waves of stares began to touch me; first I felt it with the children, and later with the lady of the house. They aren't indifferent, it turned out. But my dreams in those days were shamefully wild. I know that dreams speak vainly. Nevertheless, their power was evil and great. In my dreams it was only I and the master of the house sitting at a table, drinking glass after glass. His touch was not like the Ruthenians'. He caressed my neck gently. So it was, night after night.

I had other dreams too, harder to bear than those, that would terrify me like the sights of the church on fast days. In my dreams, I saw a flock of Jews standing at the mouth of a pit. Strong lights were aimed at them, but they stood their ground, not moving. We have killed Jesus once and for all, and we won't permit his resurrection; their eyes were furious. The strong lights kneaded their flesh, and they stood their ground, as though they had become a single mass, blocking the entrance.

These sights have not been erased from my memory. Even

today I remember them with great clarity. In those dreams I knew all my sins. Not only had I left my ancestors and their land, I had abandoned my daughter and, to add insult to injury, I was living among those who had raised their hand against God and His Messiah. I knew that my punishment would be too heavy to bear, not only in the world of truth but first of all here too, on this earth.

I considered abandoning the house and going wherever my legs would carry me, but I was weak, afraid, and everything around me seemed alien and neglected. My friends in the tavern didn't let up: "You must leave those accursed people." "It's better to starve." "You don't know what they've done to you."

"A lot of people work for the Jews." I tried not to get upset.

"But you've changed."

"They don't do me any harm."

"You don't know. They work silently, secretly. They change you from the inside. Those fiends are clever and smart, and one day you're going to get up, and you'll see: You're tainted with Jewish leprosy. What'll you do? Who'll take you in? No young fellow will want to sleep with you. Where will you go then? Where?"

They rebuked me in that manner.

In the end they were right: Fear gradually overcame me. Not a distinct fright but a dread that gnawed from within. I kept working, eating, and sleeping, but everything I did was tinged with fear. More than once I saw with my own eyes the whirling sword over my head.

One night I left the house and ran away. It was the end

of October. The cold and the darkness blew through the empty streets. I felt I was losing my mind, and I could do no more. Fear drew me inward, into the tunnels of damp and cold. After walking for an hour I felt relief. My feet were wet and my body was cold, but I wasn't sorry. Joy suffused me, as though I had been released from prison.

The tavern was locked that night, so I headed toward the railway station. At the station I didn't find anyone I knew. A few drunks were lying in the corners, grunting merrily. For a moment I wanted to join them in a drink.

"Why don't you come over to us, it's warm here," one of the drunks called to me. I knew that was no summons from on high but an earthly call, clumsy and evil, but I was still glad to hear the Ruthenian language, my mother tongue. I stood where I was and drew no closer.

"Come over to us, and we'll have a drink. Where do you work, darling?"

"For the Jews," I said, and immediately regretted that I had revealed my secret.

"Damn them, it's good you left. Liberty is as necessary for us as the air we breathe." That sudden, coarse contact with my mother tongue brought a thrill of pleasure to my body. They grunted, shouted, and whinnied out loud. As though by enchantment, those clumsy noises reminded me of the tranquil meadows of my native village, of the water and the isolated rows of trees planted on the broad plain and scattering shadows with a generous hand.

Only now did I realize how detached I had become from the good soil, from my late mother, from the light of grace that had encircled me in distant days. The drunks seemed to guess what I was thinking, and they called out again: "It's good you left those cursed ones. It's better to go hungry and not take shelter under their roofs."

Now I knew clearly what they were talking about. In that neglected, filthy place, which everyone called the central railroad station, I felt for the first time that a Jewish mood had penetrated my bones and destroyed my joy in life.

"Why don't you come over to us? What harm have we done?" they called again.

"I have to go back to work."

"You don't have to go back. By no means. The Jews are cursed. They've already enslaved you."

"They've done me no harm."

"If that's what you think, you're stupid."

When I drew close to them, the sight struck me in the face. The drunks were lolling in rags, bottles, and scraps of food like beasts. The thought that soon I would be among them froze me. "Leave me alone," I screamed, shackled as if in a nightmare.

"Stupid girl," one of them called, and threw a bottle at me. "Those cursed ones have already enslaved you. You're trapped in their net, you stupid thing. You had something, not much, and that's just what they took from you. You don't know, stupid, but we know already. You'll end up regretting your life."

I went out into the streets and wandered all night long. My heart screamed: Jesus, Jesus, save me the way You have always saved all sinful women. Gather me up together with them, and don't let me die in my sin. The night was cold, and I tramped through the streets, from alley to alley, from square to square. If the angel of death had come and taken me, I would have thanked him, but the redeemer didn't come, only darkness, all shades of darkness, and all kinds of cold.

If no one wants me, I'll go back to the Jews. Jesus would also have returned to them, I said to myself, but the fear was fiercer than I was.

Finally, the rain made the decision for me. Rain mingled with hail fell toward the morning and forced me inside. I opened the door. The house was sunk in deep sleep, and everything was in its place. On all fours, I crept to my bed.

6

"YOUR EYES ARE RED," said the mistress of the house.

"Dreams tormented me," I lied.

Meanwhile, life resumed its open course: rising, tidying the house, washing, and ironing. During pauses or at night, I used to tell the boys about my home, about the meadows and the rivers, all the beloved things preserved within me from my childhood. But so they wouldn't think that everything was quiet and pleasant, I rolled up my sleeves and showed them the scars on my arms.

More than once I observed them in their sleep and said to myself: Dear Lord, they're so frail. Who will defend them in a time of trouble? Everybody hates them, and everybody wants to harm them. More than once I spoke about it to them. Boys of their age in the village ride on horseback, go out to the pasture, sharpen scythes. Ten-year-olds are like twenty-year-olds, with their hands in everything. They swim in the river and drift on rafts, and when they need to, they join in fights. When I told them about all those wonders, they looked at me very attentively and wonderingly but without fear. They, apparently, knew what to expect in the future. They were prepared for it. Talking with them, in any event, always amused me: They learn to ask at an early age. I didn't mind if they asked. I told them about everything. My stories made them laugh and amazed them. They asked about details, sometimes about the tiniest details.

For amusement, I too began asking. They were miserly in their answers. Don't talk too much. That's a general rule that the Jews are very strict about. I had also learned how to be quiet, for a different reason. My mother beat me several times for shooting off my mouth. Since then, it's been hard for me to talk.

Meanwhile, I received greetings from my village. My cousin Karil looked for and found me. The winter rains were bad, the harvests were meager, illness had spread among the cattle. My old father needed a little money now. Karil spoke in a temperate and serious voice. I undid my kerchief and gave him everything I had. "Have you any more?" he asked.

"That's what I have."

"When will you have more?"

"In a month or two, when they give me."

"Honor thy father and thy mother." My old cousin found the proper occasion to preach a moral lesson to me. He also added, "Honor not only with speech but also with money." The way the peasants use verses from the Bible makes me laugh.

In that short time, my cousin managed to tell me that my father's wife wasn't as good as my mother. She was lazy, pretended to be sick, and last summer they hadn't seen her in the field. The details recounted in his stories brought my native village before my eyes, my father and my mother. Now I felt the strangeness that had been suspended between myself and them, as though a yawning abyss and a black river separated us. Almighty God, what happened? I wanted to scream. All that beloved green was once mine. What had seized it from me? I didn't know then that my few years in town had molded me, changed me, and all the possessions I had brought from my ancestors' house were lost. But never mind. I had received far more, more than I was worthy of. The Jews didn't abandon me. I was with them all along the way.

The next day the cold sun shone and the mistress of the house announced to me: Passover is coming. Who still remembers a Jewish Passover here? I'm the last one, it seems to me. Those weren't easy days for me: I worked hard; I scoured pots with sand. Afterward, I used to dip them in a barrel of boiling water, to scorch them. Those smells are still encased within me like hidden secrets. Years in the service of the Jews are no laughing matter. The Jewish odor is a complex affair. In my childhood, I heard people say that the Jews smell of soap. That's a lie. Every one of their days and every one of their holidays has its own smell, but particularly pungent are the aromas of Passover. For many years I lived in the midst of those fragrances.

Passover has many odors, but for me the flowers of spring became flowers of mourning. On the second day of Passover, in the middle of the street, the master of my house was murdered. A thug attacked him and stabbed him to death. Every Passover they kill a Jew, sometimes two. I heard afterward in the tavern how he was killed. One of the toughs decided the master of my house would be the victim that year, because he had refused to sell to a peasant on credit. That was only an excuse, of course. Every Passover they make a sacrifice. This time the lot fell upon Benjamin.

Thus, in broad daylight, my beloved was murdered. Forgive me, Jesus, if I say something that won't please You, for if there was one man whom I loved in my lifetime, it was the Jew Benjamin. I have loved many Jews in my life, rich Jews and poor Jews, Jews who remembered they were Jews and those who tried to forget. Years passed before I learned to love them properly. Many hindrances prevented me from drawing close to them, but you, Benjamin, if I may address you personally, laid the foundation for my great love, you, in whose eyes I did not even dare look, whose prayers I heard from a distance, and it's doubtful whether I ever entered your thoughts even once. You taught me to love.

In their burial arrangements, as in other ritual matters, the Jews are frightfully practical. All their pain and mourning are without a melody, without a flag, and without a flower. They lay the body in the grave and rapidly cover it, without delay.

The next day, after the funeral, I was sure all the Jews would gather up their belongings and flee. I too felt a fear of death, but to my surprise, no one left the city. The lady of the house sat on the floor with her two children, and the house filled with people. The weeping was scant, no one cursed, and no one raised his hand against his fellow man. God has given and God has taken away; that's the verse, and that's the moral. The common opinion that the Jews are cowards is baseless. People who lay their dead in an open pit, without decoration and without glory, are not cowards.

I stayed secluded so that no one would see my mourning. Thoughts tortured me all week long: the sight of my mother's face and of the face of Jesus. But more clearly than anyone I saw Benjamin—not a ghost, but as I had seen him for five years, sitting at the table, his face turned inward, but illuminated.

After the week of mourning, Rosa got up and went to the store; the children returned to school. Benjamin's death accompanied me everywhere. Had I not been afraid, I would have gone and thrown myself on his tomb. That concealed mourning sent me back to the tavern. I had a few drinks. I didn't get drunk; I came home foggy. On the way, one of my Ruthenian acquaintances met me and proposed that we spend the night together.

"I'm sick," I told him.

"What's the matter with you?"

"I don't know."

"Why don't you leave the Jews?"

"They're good to me."

He twisted his face into an expression of contempt, repugnance, and disgust. He spat and turned away. That was the end of my intimate relations with my fellow Ruthenians. Within my soul I decided that I wouldn't leave the house, even if my salary was low, from now on. Benjamin's death brought me close to his wife, Rosa. We used to talk a lot about the boys, insults, and wounds. The Jews don't indulge in idle talk, but Rosa, in her time of suffering, drew close.

More than once we would stay deep in conversation until late at night.

Thus I bound my soul up with theirs. I raised the children as though they were my own. Rosa trusted me, and she didn't lock the cabinets or dressers. The division of labor was simple. She worked in the store, and I worked at home. The children studied and got on excellently, and along with her, I felt pleased at their every success.

I used to flee my former friends, but they pursued me everywhere, and always with the same question: "What's the matter with you, Katerina?"

"Nothing at all," I decided to answer.

Sometimes I used to go into the tavern, sip a drink or two, but I didn't sit for a long time. Life in my native village fell further behind me. I continued going to church, but only on holidays. The Jews are evil, the Jews are corrupt, they must be rooted out, I would hear on every corner. That muttering reminded me of winter in the village. The young men in the village used to organize to hunt Jews. For many days they would talk about it and laugh. The hunt included horses, dogs, and scarecrows, and in the end they used to haul an old Jew into the village, torment him, and threaten to put him to death because he had killed Jesus. The old man would beg for his life, and finally, he would have to pay his own ransom in cash, standing in shock for a long time after the ordeal.

Meanwhile, I learned that my father had passed away. No one bothered to inform me. A peasant from the village who I happened to meet told me. When I returned home and told Rosa, she told me, "Take off your shoes and sit on the floor and mourn for your father as if he had died today."

"My father didn't love me."

"That makes no difference. We are commanded to honor our fathers." That answer astounded me with its simplicity. I took off my shoes and sat. Rosa gave me a cup of coffee. I didn't mourn for my father, may God forgive me, but for my secret love.

Abraham and Meir taught me to read, and I am very grateful to them. There's no greater pleasure than reading. I open a book and gates of light are open before me. My mother tongue grew impoverished in my mouth, and when I talk with a peasant, I mix a few words of Yiddish in with my language. The peasant laughs and asks, "Where are you from?" And when I tell him that I'm a Ruthenian, a village girl, he reprimands me. One peasant cursed me out loud, calling me a witch, worse than the devil.

True, after Benjamin's death I grew thinner. My gait wasn't as firm as before, food that wasn't Jewish was hard for me to digest, vodka gave me heartburn, but I wasn't weak or sick. True, many dreams filled my sleep, and that's not a good sign. All dreams augur ill. Sometimes it seemed to me that I saw black angels and sometimes birds of prey. When I awoke, the smell of blood surrounded me on all sides. The dreams returned night after night. I hadn't told Rosa about them, but finally I could no longer withhold them, and I told her. Rosa's response surprised me: "What do you want? They always lie in wait for us."

Apparently, she didn't know how right she was. At Hanukkah, hooligans burst out of the tavern and ransacked

Jewish stores. The snow was deep, roads were cut off, and the cry for help went unheard. The toughs did their bloody work without hindrance. They didn't spare women or old people. Their cries rose up to the heavens, but no one came to their aid.

The next day the police counted twenty-one dead, including three children. Rosa had protected her little store with fierce tenacity, but the hooligans were stronger than she was and they strangled her.

I shall never forget that funeral in the snow. The dead outnumbered their mourners. Snow fell without letup, and the silence was like ice. The peasants shut themselves up in their homes like wild beasts in their lairs. I hugged the children to my breast and swore on Rosa's grave that I wouldn't abandon them.

Sometimes it seems that time has stopped its flow: I am still at home, by the sink, washing their shirts, polishing their shoes, and escorting them to school. The air outdoors is clear. The years have only sharpened its clarity. My love for Benjamin did not flag and wasn't forgotten. I see him sometimes very distinctly, but Rosa is closer to me, like a sister. With her I can converse at any time, for hours. And always, it is as though she is sitting by my side. A kind of untarnished practicality. Once, I was unable to value that forthrightness properly. Now I know, you, my dear ones, are my root on this earth. I have served in many homes during my long life, I have loved many people and some of them loved me, but from you, Rosa, I drew strength and patience.

Now, almighty God, no other soul is close to me on this earth. They've all perished in horrible deaths. Now they are

stored up only within me. At night I feel them. They crowd
in close to me, together, and with all my strength I try to
protect them. All the people around here are informers and
wicked. No one is upright and no one is merciful.

Sometimes I hear their voices, quiet, but very clear. I
understand every word. The link hasn't been severed, thank
God, and we continue our long summer conversations, the
good winter conversations, and you, my sons, Abraham and
Meir, your ironed uniforms, your briefcases strapped to your
backs, your fine report cards—you're all within me. The
years have not made you part from me. Now I am here and
you are there, but not far away and not estranged.

7

Autumn came on time, and Chamilio brought me two baskets of provisions. His expression is mute and concentrated, as if his will has been completely effaced. His closeness embarrasses me. And though he's barely human any longer, he's more than human. Thank you, Chamilio, for taking such trouble. God bless you, I want to shout out loud. He puts the provisions down in the pantry and goes out to chop firewood for me.

The autumn is showing itself in my legs. The rain isn't abundant, but it's constant. Without a stove lit, a person could freeze in his house. For a long while Chamilio toils at arranging the house. In the end he leaves without saying anything. "My angel, many thanks to you," I call to him with all my strength. Now, for some reason, it seems to me that he has caught my shout.

For entire days I am alone. I light the stove, and the smell of the wood on the fire brings me back to the scattered regions of my life. Again I am in Strassov, the orphans are with me, everyone deep in mourning, and no one comes to visit. A moist silence swaddles us together on the floor. At night hooligans run riot in the street and shout: "Death to the merchants, death to the Jews." Weiss's leather shop has been smashed open all along the front, the merchandise stolen, but the smell of leather remains and wafts up from it. The odor drives me out of my mind.

The last days, I felt, had changed me. A kind of trembling coursed through my fingers, and I knew that if one of those toughs broke in, I'd deal with him the way my father would have. I wouldn't hesitate to stick a knife into him. Nevertheless, I decided that I wouldn't test myself. I gathered up a few clothes and, without asking anyone's permission, set out for the country with the boys.

Two pale Jews were standing next to the wall of the house. Fear had congealed on their faces and on their long coats. "Why don't you clear out?" I pleaded. My cry didn't make them budge. They looked like sick animals, sunk and hypnotized in the slumber of death.

I reached the village at noon. A small village, clinging to the hilltops, not like my native village, where the houses sag in the valley and the mud. Here the hills smile, the ravines are broad and open, and the snow reclines calmly, bright and soft.

Right away I rented a house, a low house, made of thick wooden beams, topped with a thatched roof. "The windows are wide but well sealed; there's plenty of wood for heat," said the landlord, happy at the unexpected deal.

"Were there riots here?" I asked.

"Nothing. Its been a normal winter."

The children slept, and I secretly burrowed into their sleep. I went out for supplies only once a week. I was careful

not to eat nonkosher food, promising Rosa I would watch
over the boys so that not a speck of impurity would cling
to them. In my heart I knew it was a false promise. Ru-
thenianism prevailed over everything here, over me too. The
sight of winter captivated me with its charms. What could
I do? "What shall I make?" I asked, and in my heart I knew
that everything here—the stove and the dishes, the bread
and the oil, every inch of the floor, the smell of linen, everything, even the bedclothes—was *tref.*

"What shall I make?" I asked again.

"It doesn't matter," said Abraham, the elder, relieving me
from my hesitations.

Thus began our life here. It was a long winter, most of
which we spent in the broad peasant bed. The stove roared
and released its heat into the thin darkness. The boys quickly
discovered the pleasures of the Ruthenian language. At first
they spoke hesitantly, but later they became accustomed to
it. I answered them in Yiddish and warned them in a voice
not my own that they must retain their language and that
forgetfulness was very powerful here.

The winter deepened and left me speechless. Vodka would
draw me out of my silence for a moment. I didn't drink a
lot, but the little that I sipped rooted out fear and restored
words to me. I spoke with the boys about the need to be
strong and to strike at the wicked without fear. I knew there
was a flaw in my speech, but I couldn't hold my tongue.
My bold mother, my bitter mother, was speaking from
within me. That winter, may God forgive me, I loved the
children and hated the Jews. And if I fed them *tref,* I meant
only to strengthen them. One evening I showed them the
butcher knife and told them that it was our weapon in times

of trouble. We mustn't fear. Against the wicked one must struggle with all one's might. I was drunk, of course.

The warm winds came early and imperceptibly crumbled the mountains of snow. Masses of ice fell into the ravines and smashed with deafening thunder. At night the house shook. I knew it was a sign from above, but I didn't know its meaning.

Before long, spring rose from the dead snow. It was a muddy, damp spring, kneaded together as though by itself. These labor pains lasted a month, and finally the fog expired and the sun bathed the house and the yard in warm light.

The boys worked with me in the vegetable beds. The sun beat down pleasantly from the early morning hours till dark. The day would slip by in the wink of an eye. At night I would cook mamaliga with cheese, a bowl of milk, and hard-boiled eggs. Our appetites were strong, the touch of darkness was pleasant, and sleep was deep.

The boys grew taller and their skin tanned. In my heart, I knew that Rosa wouldn't be happy at the sight of her boys in the vegetable garden. But I, or rather the evil spirit within me, said: You must be sturdy. Sturdy people give back blow for blow. Frightened Jews arouse the devils.

In those summery expanses a person easily becomes addicted to the sights, the pleasant water, and the flat, soft grass. My life was limited, but it was full of strength. At night I would collapse beside the boys, and my hand seemed to want to make the sign of the cross. I knew that something wasn't right, but what exactly was wrong, I didn't know. The children grew forgetful together with me. The days grew longer, and at night we used to sit on a ledge and gobble watermelons.

During that long, marvelous summer, may God forgive me, I forgot Rosa more than once. I didn't remind the boys about their duties and I didn't insist that they pray. After a day of work they would race over the hills like the peasants' children. Often, I sinned by lying. I promised them that one day we would return to the city and the Jews. They didn't ask many questions, and I didn't offer any answers. I knew—at every moment I knew—that this pleasure wouldn't last long, but I ignored evil thoughts and fears. I worked in the field. I washed. I ironed. I was sure, in my innocence, that those deeds had the power to hide me from evil eyes.

While the summer was at its height, as in the midst of a nightmare, Rosa's sister-in-law appeared, a broad, sturdy woman, accompanied by two Ruthenian thugs. She stood at the door of the cabin, and my body froze. "Where have you been?" she addressed the boys as if I didn't exist. The boys were dumbstruck. Then she addressed me, and with a voice I hadn't heard since my mother died, a mixture of anger and choking, she said: "Why did you kidnap the children? It's forbidden to kidnap children. Everybody trusted you. And this is the reward we get?"

Blood boiled in my veins, but my words were stifled. It was like long ago in the field, when my mother would ambush me and beat me till I bled. This time it wasn't a hand striking me but a mouth. She immediately turned to the boys with a false smile and said, "We haven't forgotten you. We've been looking for you everywhere. We've searched every nook and cranny." The boys didn't utter a word. They drew near and huddled close to me, their closeness freeing me from my silence. I opened my mouth and said, "Why are you making false accusations against me? I've watched over the boys. Rosa's sons are as dear to me as my own children. Let the boys speak for themselves!"

The boys remained at my side and trembled.

She ignored me. "Don't you recognize Aunt Frantzi?" she said to the boys in a thick, discordant voice.

I was immobilized, like in a dream. Everyone seemed taller and stronger than I. I turned to the husky Ruthenians and said: "Don't believe her. She's leading you astray."

"Kidnapper. Keep quiet!" She heard me and roused herself.

"Damn you!" The sound escaped from within me.

The Ruthenians approached me and told me that the Jews were paying them six thousand in cash for every missing person they located. "What do you need those boys for? We'll give you a new coat and galoshes from Germany." They spoke to me in my language, like brother to sister.

Meanwhile, the woman squatted down and was speaking to the children. Her words were like nails in my flesh.

Leave them be, I wanted to shout.

"Take your belongings and let's go," one of the Ruthenians said to the boys.

That direct address frightened the children, and they clung closer to me.

"We want to return you to your family."

"I want Katerina." Meir burst into tears.

"Katerina isn't your mother, and she's not even your aunt."

Now the aunt spoke to them: "You mustn't forget that you're Jews. Your mother is in the world of truth, and she has no peace. For two months now I've been dragging my legs from place to place."

"We want Katerina," wailed Meir again.

"You mustn't talk that way. Your aunt has come to save you. You're Jews. You mustn't forget that you're Jews."

"Why are you talking to him? Why are you begging?" One of the Ruthenians said. "Let's just take them."

"Don't take them by force." The words left my mouth.

The Ruthenian's patience snapped. "We do our best. But if people don't understand, there's no choice. What do you want, for us to beg?"

"Boys," I said, and my voice was choked in my throat. "You decide. I don't want to interfere."

"We'll stay with you," said Abraham, who hadn't yet uttered a word.

"What are you talking about?" the Ruthenian said to him roughly. "You have to go back. Your place is with the Jews. This woman has taken care of you, but now you're going home. Is that clear?"

For a moment I was about to implore the Ruthenians, my countrymen, and tell them that these children were more precious than anything to me. I had brought them up, and without them my life was not worth living. But I understood that they wouldn't give up their reward and my plea would be in vain.

All at once, the boys leaped away and began running toward the forest. Within seconds, they had disappeared. "What did you do to them?" The woman was shaken, but the two Ruthenians weren't flustered. They ran to the top of a hill and split up. A chill went through my body at the sight of their sturdy approach. They advanced slowly, with graceful steps. At the edge of the woods, they leaped into the vegetation like wolves.

"What did you do to them?" The woman spoke to me again, gritting her teeth. "Why did they flee?"

"I don't know. I'm not a witch." I poured my fury into that last word. The woman apparently sensed my anger and said, "I'm their aunt. The obligation to raise them and educate them falls upon me. For two months now I've been dragging myself around. Why didn't you bring them to us?"

"I was afraid." I revealed a piece of the truth.

That single phrase took effect. The woman buried her face in her two hands and burst into weeping. I now knew very clearly that I had adopted the boys in the past two seasons. No one could sunder that tie.

Meanwhile, the woman shook off her tears: "I've walked on foot from village to village. Finally, the Jews had pity on me and hired the two Ruthenians so they would find the boys. I didn't believe in them, but they knew where to look."

I was weak, and in my great weakness I said, "The boys prayed every morning."

"Thank you. I thank you from my heart," the woman said distractedly. "They prayed, you say?"

"Yes."

"Thank God, not everything is black." The dread was shed from her face for a moment, and she added, "It's hard to drag yourself from place to place. My legs swelled up. But there are things that are more important than your life. You must repeat that to yourself sometimes. More than once I said to myself, Let this weak body rest a little. Thank God

I overcame that temptation. What did the children do all the time?"

"They played in the yard."

"And you didn't say anything to them?"

"What could I say?"

In my heart, I knew that the boys' fate was sealed. Nothing escapes the wolf's fangs, and those Ruthenians were worse than wolves. They wouldn't leave the thicket empty-handed. But secretly, may God forgive me, I was glad of the boys' courage. That was a sign that I had planted something of myself inside of them.

"Where are they?" The woman roused herself from her lethargy. "You know the forest."

I overcame my repugnance and examined her closely. She was about forty, her hair was thin, and two pink creases crossed her forehead. She had once been sturdy, apparently. Now her legs were swollen and she could barely stand. "Rosa has left us," she continued to mutter. "May her merit protect the boys. I can't drag my legs anymore."

Evening fell, but the sky didn't get dark. The lights of the sunset glowed on the treetops. "Where are they? I'm their aunt. It's my duty. Why did they run away from me? I'm not a monster."

Don't worry, they'll find them, I was about to tell her, but it was unnecessary. Broken cries, stifled cries, were heard from the forest. Within seconds the shouts became choked weeping.

The Ruthenians came out of the forest, waving their prey in their hands like rabbits. "Sons of bitches." My ear caught their words before they threw the boys into the deep bed of the wagon. The woman rose from where she lay and ran to them with a kind of clumsy haste, like someone who has learned of a disaster. The two Ruthenians stood by one of the horses and their stance bespoke a coarse satisfaction.

"Where are the boys?" the woman asked stupidly.

She climbed in on all fours and grasped the beams. The Ruthenians jumped on, and, without saying anything, they snapped their whips. The draft horses lifted their legs and were swallowed in the darkness.

I collapsed like a building beneath which the foundation has been taken away. For a long while I tried to force myself into the house, but my body was heavy and my strength had ebbed away.

8

THE FOLLOWING DAY I ROSE EARLY, packed my few belongings and, without delay, set out on my way. The autumn winds were already blowing strongly, but the sky was blue. All that had happened the day before seemed erased from my memory. My body felt as hollow as after a night of drinking.

In the afternoon it brightened up and I sat beneath a tree. A puppy attached itself to me, and I played with it. Afterward, I was of a mind to go down to the river and have a swim, but I immediately changed my mind. I rose to my feet and turned back to the high road.

As evening cast its cold shadows on the fields, I saw once again, as if onstage, the two tall Ruthenians who had come in secret and stood in the courtyard. Nor did that woman vanish from my vision, her clumsy body and her swollen legs and her repeated question, "Who taught you Yiddish?" Finally, I hadn't been able to restrain myself and I told her, "Nothing Jewish is strange to me." She apparently sensed my anger and asked nothing more.

That very night I sat in the Fieldmouse and sipped a few drinks. The streets were as bright as the day of my first arrival here. I was tired, and my fingers trembled. Since I'd last been there, the crowd had changed. The usual drunkards had gone and their place had been taken by new ones. While I was seeking familiar faces, I saw my cousin Maria. I hadn't seen her for years. She was unchanged—the same brazen look, the same vigorous vitality. I hugged her to my breast, and all my humiliations rose up before me. Maria seemed to sense my loss. She held and kissed me, and right then and there she announced, "A dinner fit for a king."

"Where are you?"

"With the Jews."

"It's hard for me to work for Jews more than a month."

"Why?"

"They irritate me."

Since my childhood, every time I'd been depressed, Maria pulled me out of it. Danger meant nothing to her. She leaped off a bridge into the river like the fishermen, rode on horses, sailed rafts, and shouted out loud, "Son of a bitch!" If something struck her mind, she'd do it without hesitation.

"Where are you heading?" I asked.

"I'm going away in two hours."

"Where?"

"To Vienna."

She'd gotten in trouble more than once and again needed a gynecologist. Yet she emerged from all her travails stronger and more audacious.

"I'm tired of everyone. I need new sights now," she exclaimed.

I envied her, because my own will is flinched. For a moment I was about to say, I'll go too, but I sensed that I wasn't ready yet for journeys like that. Maria had only to wish and she could spread her wings and take off.

We ate a good dinner. Suddenly, I saw my village before me, the meadows and the cattle and Mother standing by the dairy gate with a pitchfork in her hand, sharp contempt compressed in her eyes. It was clear she felt contempt not only for her husband and sisters-in-law but also for her childhood friends who had become rich and now ignored her. Something of that look now flickered in Maria's eyes.

I walked her to the train platform. Now I knew that if it hadn't been for Maria, it was doubtful whether I'd have left the village. She looked at me kindly but without pity, and she said, "You mustn't be discouraged. You must learn to listen to your desires and not consider anyone else. People who are too considerate fall flat on their faces in the end. If you've decided to steal, then steal. If a fellow pleases you, sleep with him right away. The true will knows no bounds."

That's how Maria was. I accompanied her up the ramp and cried. My heart told me I would never see her again. Many people have been wiped out of my memory, but not Maria. She is ensconced in my heart, and I think about her often. To her credit, it should be said that she never offered false consolations. She demanded courage from everyone, even from the weak. She was contemptuous of the Jews because they love life, they cling to life at any price. "If you don't risk your life, it isn't worth living," she used to say.

I parted from Maria, and the light went out above me all at once. If the old conductor had come up and said to me,

"Come to my lodge and warm up my bones," I would have gone with him. There was no will in me. I collapsed in a corner and fell asleep.

The next morning was cold and clear, and I had severe heartburn. A few drunkards clustered in a corner and cursed the income tax office and the Jews. At their stands, Jews sold candies wrapped in luscious pink paper.

"I'm not afraid," said one of the old Jews, removing himself from a slit in the wall.

"I'll be back," the thug threatened him.

"Death doesn't frighten me anymore."

"We'll see."

"I'm going to death with my eyes open." The Jew left his niche and stood up straight on the sidewalk.

"Why are you shaking?"

"I'm not shaking. You can come and see."

"You disgust me."

"You're not a human being. You're a beast of prey," said the Jew, and he didn't rush back to his hole.

I had neither friends nor relatives here. My purse shrank and emptied. I stood in the busy railroad station as on the day of my arrival here. My mother tongue evoked a hidden sight within me: my mother's funeral. Often I promised myself to return to the village and kneel on my parents' graves, but I didn't keep that promise. My native village always had frightened me, and now even more so. Soon, I curled up in a corner and fell asleep. In a dream I saw Rosa sitting in the kitchen and clutching a cup of tea in her palm. A cold light poured over her forehead, her cheekbones jutted out, and her gray hair was not covered by a kerchief. There was no beauty in her face, just a strange restfulness.

The next day I was standing, lost in the mass, and a woman approached me and said, "Perhaps you'd like to work for me." After days of wandering, struggle, and despair, once again an angel had appeared from on high. God almighty, only miracles happen to me. Every day the miracles are renewed and I, in my haste, had said that there was only ugliness here, only darkness.

She was a tall woman, with measured movements, very pretty, like a heroine of the Polish nobility. For a moment I was pleased that fortune had favored me with a different face this time. A Jewish home is a quiet one but very strict.

"Where have you worked until now?"

I told her.

"I too, if you don't mind, am Jewish."

I was astonished and, greatly embarrassed, I said, "I'm familiar with the laws of *kashrut*."

"We are Jews of course, but we don't observe the commandments."

I didn't know what to answer, so I said, "As you wish."

It was a spacious home, different from regular Jewish households. In the living room stood a piano, and there was a bookcase in every room. Here, no one recited blessings and no one prayed, and in the kitchen there was no separation between milk and meat. Here, they only insisted on one thing—quiet. "There are also other kinds of Jews," Maria's mother had once informed me. "Free-thinking Jews. I don't like them. The Orthodox Jews are a little coarse, but they're stable." Then I didn't understand what she was talking about.

"My name is Henni, and I'm a pianist," she introduced herself. "Don't call me madam or Miss Trauer, and don't address me formally. Call me Henni, and I'll be very grateful to you."

"As you wish."

"We eat very little meat but a lot of fruit and vegetables. The market isn't far. Here's the pantry, and these are the pots and pans. I have no time for anything. I'm a slave, as you'll see. What else? That seems to be everything."

Henni practiced hour upon hour, and at night she shut herself up in her room and didn't leave till morning. With Rosa I had been used to talking, and we would discuss everything, even secrets. There were days when I had forgotten that I had been born to Christian parents, that I was baptized, and that I went to church, so immersed did I become in the Jewish way of life and their holidays, as if there were no other world. And here there was neither Sabbath nor holiday. At first this life seemed like an unbroken stretch of pleasure, but I quickly learned that Henni's life wasn't at all easy. Once a month she used to travel to Czernowitz to appear in the concert hall, and when she returned, her face would be drawn, her mood gloomy, and for days she wouldn't leave her room. Her husband, Izio, a quiet and mild-mannered man, tried to console her, but words were of no use. She was mad at herself.

"Henni, why are you angry?" I dared to ask.

"My performance was terrible, beneath contempt."

"Who said so?"

"I did."

"A person mustn't blame himself." I used one of Rosa's expressions.

"That's easy to say."

So she dismissed me. It was hard for me to get close to her. I didn't understand her. In the village I had never met women like that, and Rosa was different. Sometimes, after many hours of playing the piano, she would come to me and, somewhat distractedly, say, "Katerina, I thank you very much for your service. I'm giving you an extra hundred. If it weren't for you, I wouldn't have a home. You're my home."

Before the holidays, Henni's mother used to appear, a tall and powerful woman, casting dread on everyone. The old mother was very Orthodox and anguished by her daughter's way of life. She addressed me directly, saying, "My daughter, to my heartfelt regret, has forgotten her origins. Her husband is no better than she is. You must do that which is pleasing to God."

Immediately, she ordered me to take all the pots and pans out of the cupboards, to boil a large pot of water, and to prepare sand and lye. Henni shut herself up in her room and didn't leave it. The old mother was glad that the laws of *kashrut* weren't unfamiliar to me, and in her great joy she hugged me and said, "I'm glad I have someone in this world who understands me. My daughter doesn't. She thinks I'm mad. By your grace, Katerina, you'll keep watch over the house, and I'll pay you fully for being on guard. What can I do? Concerts are more important to my daughter than a kosher home."

For a week we worked to purify the house. At the end of that time, the kitchen was divided into dairy and meat sections, according to the rules. The old mother gave me a banknote worth two hundred and said, "This is a lot of money, but I trust you. My daughter is living in sin, and I can't do anything about it. Everything she does is only to make me angry. If you keep watch over the kitchen, perhaps the kosher food will kindle good thoughts in her."

Later, she approached the door of her daughter's room and called out, "Henni, Henni, I organized the kitchen together with Katerina. I'm going back home. Do you hear me?" No answer was heard. She mounted the coach and set out on her way.

Late at night, Henni came out of her room and said, "That's it. We've survived that steamroller, too." Just then our eyes met and my soul was bound to hers. That very night she told me that once she and her mother had been close, but in recent years her mother had been seized by religious qualms. Once every two months she would appear like a whirlwind. She was a very strong woman, and the effect of her dreads was strong, too. For some reason, it seemed to her that Henni was about to convert to Christianity.

That night I learned from Henni that Izio wasn't her husband but a childhood friend with whom she had been living for years. Izio was studying the ancient, marvelous monasteries dispersed throughout Bucovina. With the passing years, he had found pleasure not only in antiquities but also in the monks' way of life. On the weekends he would return, tired and dusty, like a tramp. That, of course, was merely what met the eye. He was entirely flooded with discoveries and experiences, and his face looked beatific.

I was happy there. The big house was at my disposal, and I strolled along its full length, with music accompanying me in every corner. Sometimes the house seemed like a church

to me, where angels soared. When Henni w
nowitz, the silence was all my own.

For entire days I was by myself, following the o
orders scrupulously. Henni sometimes joked and
"You're my rabbi, you're my Bible. Without ye ...o
would know that today was Shavuot?" For the Shavuot
festival I prepared cheese and strawberry tart: I remembered
how Rosa told me that Shavuot was a white holiday, that
the Torah was given on a day that was all light.

My cakes couldn't sweeten Henni's sadness. When Henni
returned from her trips, she was shattered and her mood
was overcast.

"Why aren't you content? What happened? All the newspapers praised your performance."

"But I, my dear, know about the flaws. Applause can't
repair deeply rooted flaws."

"Why do you torture yourself?" I couldn't restrain myself
any longer.

"That's how I am. What can I do?"

On the weekend, Izio would return from his journeys
with a bundle of books at his breast. He looked like one of
the monks ambling through silent courtyards with even, full
steps. When they reach the northern wall, they strike large
wooden mallets to remind their brothers that the hour of
prayer has come.

"Where are you going?" I heard Henni's voice.

Izio's answer shocked me. "To myself," he answered, adding nothing.

It was hard for me to understand their life together. Sometimes they seemed to be in love, and sometimes it was as if
chance had thrown them together. I, at any rate, kept my

promise and observed *kashrut*. That observance gives me great joy, as though I had returned home to Rosa and the boys.

Afterward, the old mother again descended on the house like a whirlwind. When she had ascertained that all the pots and pans were still in their place, the dairy utensils set apart from the meat utensils, she embraced me and kissed me. Henni, naturally, wasn't happy. A few days earlier she had returned from the capital tired and once more depressed. Of course, the newspapers praised her playing, but she was contemptuous of them, and now her mother had come, with all her outdated beliefs, all her fears. Because Henni wouldn't open her door, her mother sat with me and explained the whole affair: "It's all because of Izio. He corrupted her."

"He's a quiet man," I said in his favor.

"That's not quiet, it's madness. He's in love with monasteries, and I wouldn't be surprised if one day he converted from the faith of his ancestors."

Before leaving the house, she told me, "The High Holy Days are coming. Please, be gracious and remind Henni. She's lost all contact with heaven. She's completely sunk into herself. May God have mercy on her. She needs mercy very much."

The seasons passed, year pursued year, and I immersed myself in Henni's life as though it were my own. I accompanied her when she left, and I loved it when she returned. She used to come back shattered and gloomy, but I also loved her gloom. After a week of agitated sleep, we used to sit for hours. I saw with my own eyes how music was destroying her day by day, how she became intoxicated, vomited, and became intoxicated again. I hadn't the power to save her.

The disaster, or whatever you care to call it, came from another direction. Izio slumped and clung to the monasteries with a kind of morbid desire. His face changed and a greenish light covered it. The old woman turned out to be right. He went too far. The Christian faith overcame him, and one day he appeared in a monk's habit.

That very week, Henni sold the house, packed three suitcases and, without a farewell to anyone, left for Czernowitz. She paid me down to the last penny. Before leaving the house, she handed me a packet of jewelry and said, "This is for you. It will be very useful to you."

9

I WENT BACK TO THE TAVERN. Every time I left a household, I returned to the tavern. I sat by the window and before my eyes, one by one, the sights of the past days appeared to me. Two merchants had bought Henni's house after brief negotiations. Henni did not bargain hard. More than she sought to sell the house, she sought to rid herself of it. The merchants understood and quickly got her to sign a contract.

After the sale, she burst into tears. The sobbing made her whole body tremble. I wanted to say something, but nothing I could think of was appropriate. I stood like an idiot, and the longer I stood there, the more obvious my idiocy became.

"Make some vegetable soup," she said to me suddenly.

"I'll do it right away," I said, glad she had released me from the shame of silence.

We ate soup, and Henni spoke enthusiastically about the need to escape domineering managers and live a simple life, far from other people, near a forest. It was hard for me to follow what she was saying, but I sensed that she was trying to point to the error that had ruined her life and to warn me against the blindness that drags one, imperceptibly, down to destruction.

The next day Henni was on her way to Czernowitz, and I, bearing two bundles, was without a home, as on the day of my arrival here. I could have gone back to the village. Women of my age used to return to the village, marry, and have children and the slate was wiped clean. Even whores went back and got married and raised children, but I knew that I didn't belong there, and I didn't return.

I sat in the tavern and waited for a miracle. Meanwhile, there was no shortage of offensive propositions. Young peasants would attach themselves to me, make promises, threats. Once I would have slept with any lad gladly; but years of service with the Jews had changed me, apparently. Sturdy peasants now repulsed me.

"I'm sick," I lied.

"What's that matter with you?"

"My kidneys hurt."

Rumors flew from mouth to ear. Now they ignored me or kept their distance and, when they got drunk, shoved me out the door. I noticed they looked at me the way they look at a Jew: a mixture of anger and disgust.

For hours I sat and pictured Henni's face. Her presence was palpable even in her absence. Now it seemed to me that I could cling to her like a sister. But she was in Czernowitz and I was here. I sipped drink after drink and raised my spirits. With Rosa I had tried to wean myself away from drink, but my will wasn't firm. Without a drink, I trembled. Five, six drinks lifted me up out of depression and gave me the strength to live. But on days when I overdid it—and once a week I overdid it—I would joyously hallucinate. Sometimes it seemed to me that I was sitting beside my mother. My mother also liked to drink. But she always drank alone. All of her actions were done in solitude, with her teeth gritted.

In the meantime, wicked looks began to surround me. You must return to your village, the Ruthenian eyes chastised me. That was the custom in this area. If a person was sick or had lost his mind, they returned him to his native village. If the brothers couldn't bring him back, then cousins brought him back. Sometimes an anonymous Ruthenian would even perform that good deed. A Ruthenian is always a Ruthenian. If your life has gone awry, you must return to your native village and ask pardon of your dead parents, promising them that henceforth you won't leave their shelter, and if you do leave, your blood will be on your own hands.

For weeks those evil eyes pursued me. In the end I did what I intended to do: I got on the night express train and left for Czernowitz. It was my misfortune to meet my old cousin Sarina on board. She assailed me, shouting, "You've abandoned the home of your forefathers. One doesn't abandon the home of one's forefathers." I remembered her very well, an unfortunate woman, widowed at an early age. Her children didn't like her and kept their distance, and she hounded them. Once she set the priest upon her sons so that he would confront them with the duty of honoring their mother. Her years had passed in solitude and bitterness. Now she had found me.

What could I answer? I lied, of course. I told her I was going for examinations in the hospital, and when they fin-

ished the examinations, I would return home. Her mind
was set at ease, though not completely. She insisted that I
promise her and, indeed, I promised her. Along the way
she told me about my father's last days, about his illness,
and about his wife, who had tormented him. While he was
sick he had frequently mentioned my mother, the love of
his youth, which had only inflamed the wicked woman's
malice.

"She poisoned him." The words left my mouth.

"That's what people say. She didn't get off with an easy
punishment, either," Sarina spat out not without pleasure
in the other's misfortune.

After an hour's journey she stopped talking and fell asleep.
I looked up: There were no strangers, only Ruthenians and
the children of Ruthenians. Their peasant nature filled the
coach. I could understand their language and taste all the
flavors in it, and when they took a maize pie out of their
colorful baskets, I knew that food delighted their palate
more than any other delicacy. Even the odor of their coats,
the sweat of their limbs—everything, down to their
shoelaces—was close and familiar, but still a thin barrier
separated me from them. That barrier prevented me from
drawing nearer, from asking them how they were, and from
tasting their beloved foods.

"Why don't you get off with me?" Sarina asked distractedly when I woke her. She had apparently forgotten the
excuses I had heaped up. "I'll come soon," I said, and helped
her take down her packages.

"Swear." She surprised me.

I swore.

The smell of the familiar fields together with the oath

overcame me, and I wept. I wept for my loneliness and for my wanderings and for that place that had turned me out without a blessing. I remembered the two boys who had been taken from me, and the wound bled again. The railroad cars were jerked into motion, and the train sped out. My weeping eased.

At the following stations the look of things changed. A few Jews joined the voyage. I could identify Jews from far off, and it didn't matter whether they were religious or not. In my youth I had been afraid of them, but now, when I met a Jew, I felt a kind of secret affinity. You could pick them out by a number of signs: They were short and thin and loaded down with bundles. The multitude of bundles immediately made their presence conspicuous. On the trains, the peasants tried to steal from them. They pleaded and bribed, and when bribery wasn't effective, they defended their suitcases with their lives. I liked to observe them. I won't conceal it: I was drawn to them. The years in their company didn't mar that hidden attraction. They bewitched me with their gloomy smiles, but Rosa was closer to me than all of them. In her company I could talk or remain silent, it didn't matter.

While I was looking in wonder, an old Jew approached me and asked whether I would be willing to help him carry his packages from the railroad station to the tram.

"I'm willing," I said.

"I'll pay you."

"No need."

"Why? I have six heavy bundles."

"I don't need the money."

The Jew was frightened by my words and said, "I'll do

it myself." In vain I tried to persuade him. All my entreaties were useless. He stood his ground: "I'll do it myself. I always do it myself." The trust he had placed in me a moment before had apparently lapsed. When we reached Czernowitz, he tied together the six bundles and fastened them to his body and, very slowly, he dragged them to the tram.

I spent my first day in the capital in a tavern. The taverns in the capital, I must admit, are more splendid, but they're made in the same pattern: two long wooden tables with two heavy benches next to them. I had considered going directly to the city auditorium where Henni used to perform, but as was my way, I got delayed. I drank too much, and in the evening I couldn't stand. The tavern owner, for a fee, let me sleep on the floor.

The next day I located Henni, and both of us cried like little girls. Henni had become very thin, her face was gaunt, and her long dress made the bones of her shoulders project. "You need rest," I told Henni. Though she agreed with me, how could she get free of a contract for twenty-four concerts?

I knew how much I had missed her only now. By the way, I hadn't opened the packet of jewels she had given me. I had hung it around my neck, and I said to myself, This will be my talisman. Now I felt the desire to adorn myself with one of them.

Henni was in a firm and difficult humor. She made a few contemptuous remarks about Izio's becoming a monk, and finally she said, "I hate monasteries. I'll never forgive the monks for the sins they commit. A person is free."

The next day I met her manager, a young, plump Jew, grasping and fussy. He had prepared the concert tour down to the last note. To me, for some reason, that precision sounded like a banishment. You mustn't drive people from their homes, I was about to shout, but my voice didn't stand by me.

Later, we sat and sipped a few drinks. Her voice trilled. She spoke with a kind of enthusiasm of the need to overcome weaknesses and to practice a great deal, for only practice can repair the flaws. That wasn't her voice but one she had borrowed for the purposes of this conversation. What are you talking about, I wanted to stop her. You have to take care of your health, to rest in the country. But I couldn't talk. Her voice poured out and silenced me. Finally, she said, "No matter. We'll see a lot of each other, and we'll talk for many days. There's a lot to talk about. A lot."

The next day Henni left for provincial cities, and I, in my great despair, sat in a tavern and sipped a few drinks. Afterward, distractedly, I straggled along the street near the railway station. The night lights flowed on the damp sidewalks, and I, as they say, had no goal. If a man had come along and dragged me to his room, I would have gone. No one approached me. Everyone streamed by in haste. It made me angry that no one approached me, that everyone was ignoring me, but I kept on walking. For some reason I turned into a side street. While I was walking, I saw a dim light and smelled Jewish food. I had a strong desire to climb up to the first floor and ask for a little soup, but I didn't dare. I stood and waited for the door to open and for someone to call me: Katerina, come in. Why are you standing outside? For a long while I stood there. It was, it turns out, a vain expectation. One by one, the houses were shut up behind walls of darkness. "Why won't anyone give me a little soup?" I finally raised my voice. My words were not answered. The houses seemed like fortresses, and darkness was piled upon darkness. I kept on pacing, and as I continued, the odor pursued me. Irritation goaded me to climb up to the first floor and make a ruckus in front of the doors, but I didn't do it.

While I was standing there, I noticed I was in front of a small store. From the door and the lock, I knew it was a Jewish shop. I was about to pass it by and continue on my way, but something told me to stay still, and I did. Now the way inside was easy. I smashed the window with a swing of my arm, and immediately I was stuffing cigarettes and chocolates into a bag.

Furtively, I went up and continued through the alleys. I knew it was a contemptible, ugly sin, but I still felt no remorse. A coarse pleasure flooded my body. The night passed without my feeling it. I was thirsty, but all the taverns were closed. Toward morning, I collapsed in a heap at the railroad station and fell asleep.

10

I WENT FROM TAVERN TO TAVERN. The railway station street was full of them, orderly ones and some less orderly. I preferred the quiet ones. Two or three drinks restored Rosa and Benjamin to me. I know I shall never forgive myself for allowing the Ruthenians to steal the boys. Sometimes I felt they were thinking about me in secret. If I had known where they were, I would have gone to them on foot. Sometimes it seems that time has stopped and we are still together in that little shed during that winter. The rustic stove is giving off its thick heat and I am bundled up with the boys in the big wooden bed.

Each tavern evoked different sights for me. In the Royal Tavern, near the front window, I saw Henni. Now it seems to me I understand her rigor better. She couldn't bear "almost" or half measures. Without that rigor, she would have floated away. That was her character, and that was how she punished herself. Now she was jolting all over the provinces and entertaining the dull ears of the wealthy. Izio's rigor was even more severe than hers. I remember him saying, "One must peel off the many outer layers of the matter and lay bare the kernel." At that time the word *peel* astonished me. Now I understand the dread inherent in that word. I was afraid of his rigor. The Royal Tavern was quiet, and I could sit there for many hours. Once men used to accost me. Now only old men took an interest in me. In the Royal I met Sammy, a tall and husky man with eyes like a child's.

They say the Jews are cheats. Sammy, for example, didn't have an ounce of cunning. I saw him sitting in a corner, sipping a drink. In Strassov, no Jew would enter a tavern. Wonder of wonders, here a Jew sat and piled up glass after glass. I approached him. "What's a Jew doing in a tavern?"

"I like to have a drink. What can I do?"

"Jews aren't supposed to drink, don't you know?"

"I'm a sinner. What can I do?"

He looked strange in the tavern, a boy in a den of thieves.

"You mustn't be here." I spoke brazenly.

"Why?"

"Because Jews have to direct commerce. If they don't direct it, who will?"

He laughed heartily, and his laughter infected me, too.

I used to see him sometimes, but I didn't go up to him. I felt that my presence embarrassed him. Finally, he overcame it and approached me, paying me back in my own coin. "What's Katerina doing in a tavern?"

"Because Katerina is Katerina, a Ruthenian from time immemorial."

We laughed and drank like two friends.

Most of the day I wandered through the streets and slowly soaked up the big city. In fact, I didn't stray from the streets around the railroad station. But even those faded streets had the odor of a big city.

In the evening I sat with Sammy. Sammy told me about his life. Twice married and twice divorced. He divorced his first wife because she was domineering and the second because she was crazy. He had a grown daughter from his first wife, but he saw her only seldom.

"Why don't you have steady work? Every Jew has steady work."

"How do you know?" He chuckled.

"For many years I worked for Jews."

"I hope you weren't contaminated by them."

There was a kind of piercing honesty to his rejoinders. I, for my part, told him about my native village. Sammy was a stricken man, and every word that came out of his mouth was dipped in his wound. Nevertheless, a few of his movements were pleasing to the eye, and his voice, too, or rather his accent, sounded melodious to me.

I was not working then, either. I squandered the money Henni had given me with abandon. Each morning, I would wander the city streets. The city was full of Jews. For hours I sat and observed them.

In the afternoon I would enter a Jewish restaurant. My appearance astonished the customers for a moment. When I asked, in Yiddish, for chicken soup with matzoh balls, everyone's eyes opened wide, but I wasn't offended. I sat in my place, ate, and watched. Jewish foods are pleasant to

the palate; they don't have too much vinegar or an excess
of black pepper. In the evening I used to come back to the
tavern and sit beside Sammy. While he was drinking no one
did him any harm, but when he got drunk, they abused him
and called him a drunken Jew. Sammy was a strong man,
defending himself even in his drunkenness, but he didn't
have the strength to stand up to the tavern's owner, his son,
and his son-in-law. At midnight they grabbed him and threw
him out. "I won't come back here!" he shouted, but the
next day he came back.

"Get a grip on yourself," I tried to persuade him.

"I must control myself," he agreed with me.

In my heart I knew he wouldn't do it, that he couldn't
take himself in hand, but still I plagued him with vain
demands.

"And you, what about you?"

"I'm a Ruthenian, the daughter of Ruthenians. Generations of drunkards flow in my veins."

"I get drunk easily," he admitted.

The daytime was all my own. I wandered among stores,
courtyards, and synagogues, and at noon I entered the Jewish restaurant. Yiddish is a savory language. I could sit for
hours and listen to its sound. The old people's Yiddish recalled delectable winter dishes. I would sit for hours and
observe the old people's gestures. Sometimes they seemed
to me like priests who have forfeited their pride, but occasionally an old man would lift his head and direct his gaze
toward someone impertinent, and then one saw clearly the
priestly fire burning in his eyes. I, for example, loved to
stand near the window of the synagogue and listen to the

Rosh Hashanah prayers. People tell me that the Jews' prayers are maudlin. I don't hear any weeping in them. On the
contrary, they sound to me like the complaints of strong
people, firm in their opinion.

While I was wandering, doing nothing, forgetful of myself
and surrounded by many sights, I saw a large advertisement
in the newspaper: "The famous pianist Henni Trauer has
gone to her eternal rest in the resort city of Cimpulung. The
funeral will take place tomorrow morning at ten." I read,
and my eyes went dark.

I immediately went down to the railroad station to catch
the express. It was already late, the station was empty of
travelers, and only drunkards lay in the corners, making a
racket.

"Can I get to Cimpulung this evening?" I called out
desperately.

The ticket agent opened his window and said, "What's
the matter?"

"I must get to Cimpulung," I informed him.

"At this hour there are no trains to the provinces. It's
midnight, for your information."

"Not even a freight train? It doesn't matter to me. I'm
willing to travel under any condition, at any price."

"Freight trains are for beasts, not human beings."

The ticket windows shut, one after the other. The lights
dimmed. Even the drunkards collapsed in a heap and fell
asleep.

"God, send me a train from heaven," I called out. I had
barely voiced that prayer when a freight train steamed in
and stopped.

"Can I get to Cimpulung with you?" I called out to the engineer.

"Are you willing to ride with me in the cabin?"

"I'm willing."

"Climb in," he said, and lowered the ladder.

"I have a great task," I informed him. "I must get to Cimpulung."

"You'll get there," he promised.

I knew I'd have to pay the price of the trip with my body, but the trip was more important than my body. I stood in the narrow cabin, knowing what to expect.

"Why are you trembling?"

I told him that a woman who was more dear to me than a sister had suddenly died, and I had a strong wish to bid her farewell.

"We're all going to die."

My words didn't impress him.

"True, but meanwhile some set out to meet their fate and others stay alive."

"That's nothing new."

"It's hard to bear that parting." I tried to soften his heart.

But he stuck to his guns. "That's the way of the world."

I didn't know what to answer and fell silent. While he was operating the enormous engine, he asked me what village I came from. I told him at length. I wasn't afraid. I was prepared for anything to get to Cimpulung on time.

On the way, he fondled me and said, "The Jews have ruined you. You mustn't work for them."

"Why?"

"They ruin the feeling."

My heart impelled me to say, Jews are people too, but I didn't say it.

Afterward, he was busy getting the locomotive ready. He had a long conversation with the track inspector, and finally he asked him to inform all the stations he would be late. Now I saw again: Night in a railroad station is a different kind of night. The noise freezes. It isn't silence but a confined hubbub. Ever since I'd left the house, I'd known those god-forsaken places.

Later, he started the engine and spoke a lot about the Jews and the damage they caused and about the need to wipe them out.

"There are also good ones." I couldn't stand idly by.

"None." He jabbed that isolated word into the roar of the engine and added nothing.

Afterward, he stopped fondling me and, casually, said, "You've worked too long for the Jews. You mustn't work for the Jews. They ruin body and feeling." The morning steadily lit up the horizon, and suddenly it became clear to me that Henni was no longer alive. That vivid knowledge frightened me, and I wept. The engineer was busy operating the locomotive, and he paid no attention to my weeping.

Toward morning, we arrived at Cimpulung. My fear that he would take me from the station to a hotel was unfounded. He told me, not without disgust, "You're dismissed." I remembered. That was the way the manager of the restaurant in Strassov used to get rid of old women who worked for him. The morning light spread out over the empty platform. I ran for my life to a café.

The coffee was hot and thick and I sank completely into its taste. I forgot for a moment why I had dragged myself there. For a long while I sat, remembering my childhood. My father and mother now appeared very hazy, as though they had never existed. Only when I went to the cashier to pay did I remember my long night journey, and my body trembled again.

11

LIKE ALL JEWISH FUNERALS, Henni's was gloomy and confused. The people ran about next to the gate of the cemetery and spoke in panicked tones. I stood at the side. This strange tumult made my sadness congeal within me.

A tall man with an active demeanor told at annoying length about how he had learned about Henni's death at night and how he had succeeded, he and his two friends, in renting a car and arriving here. In a corner, Henni's manager spoke about disruptions of that season's programs and about the compensation he would have to pay to the owners of concert halls who had sold tickets in advance.

About ten men had gathered, and now they were waiting for the bereaved mother.

"Where can one obtain a cup of coffee? Without a cup of coffee I'm lost," called out a man dressed in an exotic coat and wearing a broad silk cravat.

"There are nothing but graves here," another man answered clearly.

"Henni will forgive me. She'll understand me. She too was addicted to coffee."

"The funeral begins at ten."

"Jewish funerals never begin on time. There's a buffet not far from here. Won't you join me?"

"I'll do it on the run."

All the faces were foreign to me; during the last year very few people had visited the house. Henni had a single sentence on her lips: "If this is your inner consciousness, if this is what your heart tells you to do, who am I to stand in your way?" She used to recite that sentence hourly. After she spoke it, there would be a silence, and then she would repeat it. That was on a Saturday when Izio hadn't returned home, and Henni knew what had been done could never be undone. She sank to the ground, moaning in tears. I, for some reason, reproached her and told her, "You mustn't weep that way for people who are still living."

Now everything had come to an end. A few Jews in tattered traditional dress scurried between the office and the graves. From time to time, they would accost someone and ask for a contribution. One of the nonreligious men said out loud, "Leave me alone," recoiling with repugnance, as though that Jew had wanted to touch him.

Time raced by, and the mother hadn't arrived. The men stood at the office door, asked questions, and grumbled. The most annoying of all was Henni's manager. He said, "We can't wait forever. There's a limit to patience."

"By all means, telephone."

"To whom? To God?"

"To her mother."

"Did they inform her?"

"I assume so."

"For whom, then, are we waiting?"

"For the mother."

"And if they didn't inform her?"

"Ask the burial society, don't ask me." The clerk's patience had snapped.

The head of the burial society didn't respond. He sat in the other room and read a newspaper.

"This is Jewish order. Jewish order is warped, confused, and wicked," said the manager, and left the office doorway.

Afterward, the manager and his two assistants burst in and demanded: "The funeral must start now. The funeral must start immediately."

"And who will pay?" The head of the burial society lay down his cards on the bare table.

"Who's supposed to pay?"

"The relatives or friends of the deceased, and if there are none—his employers. Is that too difficult to understand?"

"I, for example, don't understand it."

"It's very simple," said the head of the burial society in a voice as chilly as ice. "Maintaining the cemetery costs a fortune. Somebody has to pay, right?"

"Should the mourners pay? Now, with the dead woman lying before them?"

"There's no cause for embarrassment here. Money is money everywhere."

"And if we don't pay?"

"We'll leave the body unburied, if that's the mourners' wish."

"Now I understand," said the manager. "It's not a question of her mother but of money."

"Gravediggers have to eat too, sir. By the way, to whom have I the honor of speaking?"

"What difference does that make?"

"You don't have to tell me."

Now matters proceeded very listlessly. Neither the clerk nor the head of the burial society left the office. The sky became covered with clouds, and a thin drizzle sprinkled down. Fatigue gradually overcame me. Had it not been for the rain, I would have sat down. I tried to remember Henni's face, but I couldn't see a thing. Finally, my old cousin Sarina appeared before me. I knew she wanted to torture me, and I closed my eyes.

While we were standing there, the manager burst back into the office, shouting, "I won't wait anymore. I'm going. Cheats rule over the Jews. Everything is money. Henni was and shall always remain dear to me. I despise ceremonies. Everybody knows that I built up a magnificent career for her. You can take her body but not her spirit. She deserves another kind of funeral, a quiet one, like among the Christians. At any rate, you'll not bury me here. I'm going to have my body cremated. I don't believe in resurrection."

The officials didn't seem astonished, and they didn't react. The manager now mixed in another matter: the death of a young violinist. The violinist had died in a hotel, and the burial society had demanded an exaggerated fee for the burial.

"I see you also talk about money," said the head of the burial society, without excitement.

"I'm allowed to. I collect money for artists. Without me, there wouldn't be any art in the provinces. The provinces would languish. Who would bring young pianists here, young violinists, and famous lecturers? Who? Who pays them? You just take. You're just robbers."

"We also serve the community."

"A horrible service, a monstrous service, an evil service. I'm going. I don't want to be in the company of bloodsuckers. Come on," he said, and turned toward the exit gate. His two assistants joined him, and they went out.

"Just to avoid paying. That whole act just to avoid paying. We know your kind." The head of the burial society rose to his feet.

Now only seven people remained, neither relatives nor friends but anonymous people who had heard Henni play and been enthralled.

"Did you know the pianist?" a woman addressed me.

"I was her housemaid," I revealed immediately.

"Marvelous," said the woman. "I was present at all her concerts. She was a great pianist. It's a shame she wasted her energy traveling. An artist must appear in his native city and not wander about. In the provinces they don't know how to appreciate music. Aren't I right?"

"Death isn't the end," I told her, for some reason.

"It was easier for my father and mother. They were believing Jews and resigned to their fate, but we—how can I say it?—are different."

"Don't you believe in God?"

"I believe, and sometimes wholeheartedly, but it isn't an unbroken faith, just flashes. It's hard to explain. You speak a fine Yiddish. How did you learn it?"

"I spent most of my years with Jews."

"A strange nation, the Jews, aren't they?"

The day grew dimmer, and there was no movement. For a moment it seemed as though it would remain that way forever. We would stand there, and the clerks would sit in their office. From time to time someone would go to the door and ask a question. The official would answer or refuse to answer, and the hands of the clock wouldn't move.

While everyone was standing there, tired and mute, the head of the burial society came out of his office and announced: "The funeral of Henni Trauer will start at once. We are simple people. We never studied in academies, but we aren't corrupt; we won't leave the body unburied."

As the last word left his mouth, the gravediggers came out, bearing the coffin. What had happened, and why just now, no one inquired. The handful of people standing near the doorway hurried and ran to catch up with the gravediggers.

Prayers were rattled off, half swallowed, and it was clear to everyone that the gravediggers were doing their duty and no more. I have seen many funerals in my lifetime, but I have never seen such a hasty one as this.

After the funeral, a few beggars came out of their lairs and shouted, "Charity will save from death!" No one gave them a penny. Everyone fled the place as though from a fire.

The funeral guests dispersed, and I remained in a street bustling with people. My body was heavy, and it was hard for me to go on. That night I took refuge in a Jewish tavern. A few drunken peasants were immersed in merry chatter and didn't disturb me. I sat and drank glass after glass, and I wept.

"What's the matter?" The owner came over to me.

"I'm very tired and have no place to stay."

"No matter," the man said. "You can sleep here. I'll give you a mattress right away."

12

THE NEXT DAY THE OWNER of the tavern asked me, "Where did you pick up such a fine Yiddish?"

I told him.

"You drink too much."

"Ruthenians are used to that."

"A person who speaks such a fine Yiddish ought to quit drinking."

He won my heart. I told him about Henni's funeral, and all the grief that had been shut in my heart welled up again. I didn't linger there but went out on my way. That Jew's face accompanied me for many hours. I remembered how he had stood next to the bar, the drunkards who jokingly called him Rabbi, his silence, and the touch of his fingers. Despite the turmoil, he did his work quietly, like a man who knows that this world is merely a corridor.

The train sped through the small stations without stopping. Once again I passed the village of my birth, and my heart twinged. I knew every tree and every house. I went back and saw my mother's face again as I had not seen it for years: anger stormed her face. With that look she used to beat the animals in the stable, and with a face like that she had once called out to my father, "Fornicating son of a fornicator!" I knew that she would soon direct that look at me, and I was afraid.

For some reason, it seemed to me that everyone, including me, was still standing by that wretched office next to the cemetery and the man who had flaunted his success in arriving at the funeral on time boasted once again. The director of the burial society left his office and stood in the doorway. His round, full face expressed a kind of false forbearance—that is: If you have the time, I have the time too. I'm willing to sit here all night. If you won't pay the funeral fees, we won't bury her. You mustn't talk that way, I wanted to call out. He, apparently, sensed my intention, fixed me with his stare, and said, "Making a living comes before everything. God created us, to our regret, in the garment of bodies."

In the evening I returned to Czernowitz, tired and irritable. If I had had a room, I would have gone to bed and curled up. I entered the Royal Tavern. To my surprise I found Sammy there, merry and drunk as Lot.

"What's the matter?"

"Nothing, everything's fine, just fine." His eyes sparkled.

"You're as drunk as Lot." Something of his drunkenness infected me.

"I'm not drunk, I'm happy."

He was drunk and woozy, and to all my questions he replied, "Everything's fine, just fine. You don't know how fine it is." That blabber brought out his misery more strongly. His shirt was torn, his hair was disheveled, and his eyes were swollen and bulging, but it wasn't an ugly misery. Soft words that spoke of beautiful places and proper actions fluttered on his lips, until for a moment it seemed to me that he wasn't drunk but a believer whose belief had been strengthened from within, and now he was prepared for any trial. Later, his talk grew quieter. Suddenly, he lifted his head and said, "Tomorrow I have resolved to do some necessary things, important things."

The next day I was waiting for him, but he didn't come. I went up to the railroad station and wandered through the narrow streets. For some reason it seemed to me that I would find him there. Jewish streets reminded me of ancient streets and secrets that I'd never understand. I could wander through them for hours and observe. Sometimes the smell of a Jewish dish enfolded me and put me to sleep on the pavement.

Toward evening I found him, coming up from the ground floor of an old building, apparently his house.

"You don't have a house, I see," he said.

"I haven't."

"Come live with me."

I agreed. Sammy's apartment was a little room with a kitchen and an outside bathroom. I saw right away that his narrow window didn't absorb a lot of light, the walls were damp, and a musty smell hung in the air. In the evening we drank, but not a lot. Sammy spoke about the need to change apartments and find suitable work. He didn't complain or get angry. His face was relaxed.

He was fifty, and I was thirty. Apparently, he had once been handsome, but bad years and alcohol had ruined his body. His belly was distended, and his eyes were bloodshot and bulging. But I didn't mind. I heard softness in his voice and a desire to be good to people. Once he had been a member of the union, but he had stopped going to the meetings, because while the activists talked loudly about justice, they themselves wasted the public's money.

The next day, to my surprise, he went out to look for work. I saw how he gathered up all his forces, bound them together, and set out. I wanted to tell him, Relax, I still have money, but I didn't. It seemed to me that I mustn't spoil that great intention. He went out, and I tidied the house.

The next day, he again bound up all his willpower and went out to look for work. I knew that he was only doing it for me, and that made me sad. I, too, after cleaning the house, went out to look for work. After two rejections, I was sitting on a bench in the public park, watching the passersby. For some reason it seemed to me that the tall peasants, standing in their stalls and selling vegetables and fruit, would soon snap their whips over the heads of the Jews scurrying nearby.

An hour passed, and nothing happened. On the contrary, the peasants were enjoying the bargaining. The closeness of the Jews amused them. They talked to them in grunts, but not angrily. I went home early and washed two shirts for Sammy, an undershirt, and some socks. Sammy's shirts were dirty but didn't give off a foul smell. I hung the laundry in the courtyard.

This time Sammy returned content. He hadn't found work, but he hadn't drunk too much, either. He said to himself, "I won't fall back again." I too tried not to drink too much—two or three glasses and no more. Sammy's face surprised me by its softness. Only when he spoke about himself did it shrivel. In his youth he had wanted to sail to America. His old parents hadn't let him. He didn't dare run away. Without much thought, he had married. Marriage had made life odious for him.

The money was running out, and I was forced to sell an expensive ring Henni had given me. I went from store to store. The prices offered by the merchants were infuriatingly low. I told Sammy.

"You should know that the Jews are cheats. Money comes before everything for them," he said, with frightening composure. Finally, I found a buyer, a Jewish merchant, who paid three times the sum offered by the others. It was a valuable, good ring; he didn't conceal that from me. I was glad. Sammy and I needed a drink like a breath of air.

During that strange and happy year I dreamed that a son would be born to me. Sammy was perturbed. Children were grief to their parents and themselves. There were enough children in the world. Why add more? Meanwhile, the two of us found work for the same storekeeper. I became a cleaning woman, and Sammy worked in the warehouse. Our little happiness seemed to grow. On Saturdays we would go on excursions, venturing as far as the Prut on the tram.

On Sundays he brought a small bottle of vodka, and we would sit and drink without getting drunk.

"Weren't you ever religious?" I asked him.

"No. My parents were religious, but their piety annoyed me."

Sometimes he used to say, "You're young and pretty. You

should go back to your village and marry a rich, handsome man."

"I find you handsome."

"Why are you mocking me?"

"I swear."

My oath wasn't a vain one. He had the charm of a man whose suffering had afflicted but not destroyed him. Excessive drinking had indeed marred his features, but his face wasn't extinguished. It was possible to illuminate it with a single word. After work we used to sit for hours. Sammy burrowed into his body, and it was hard to get a word out of him. Only after two drinks did his face open, and he used to talk, even tell things.

As the days flowed on, quiet and laden, Sammy worked until five, and I was free by two. August was clear, unspotted. A kind of restlessness gripped me; trembling and severe nausea. First it seemed to me that it was a bad cold. But quickly it became clear to me I was pregnant. My heart told me that Sammy wouldn't greet this news gladly. I didn't realize then how deeply he would be wounded. In any event, I hid the news from him. I used to work until two, and afterward I went back home and prepared a hot meal. Upon Sammy's return in the evening everything was laid out. His mood got better in those days. The sickly blush, the flushed face of drunkards, was erased, and his forehead was bright.

While I was still holding myself in, hiding my pregnancy from Sammy, I met my cousin Katya in the street. She recognized me from far off and hurried toward me. For more than ten years I hadn't seen her, but she hadn't changed. The sweet wonderment of a village girl captivated by everything that crossed her path floated on her face. I held her in my arms, and immediately felt that the whole village was planted in her soft limbs.

In the village, apparently, they hadn't forgotten me. From a distance they were following my doings, and rumors, of course, weren't lacking. One of the village men had seen me with Sammy, and right away everybody knew that Katerina had taken up with a Jew.

"I would even have recognized you at night."

"I would have recognized you too, Katya."

She had married about ten years ago, and now she had two sons and a daughter, a flourishing farm, and a woodlot at the edge of the village. I had heard those facts, in the past, from Maria, and now Katya came and confirmed them. Her hearty face, her full body, and her good smile hadn't been marred over the years, an unstained freshness. I had always liked her, and now I realized how much I had liked her.

Some creatures are born under the sign of peace, peace with themselves and their parents and the place where they grew up. Katya was like that. I stood at her side, and my tongue clung to the roof of my mouth. In the end the dam burst, and I wept. Katya hugged me to her bosom and said, "Nothing's the matter. We love you the way we've always loved you." Those kind words just made me cry harder.

Later we sat in a tavern and looked at each other. Katya said, "Why don't you return home? The house is standing in its place. The land has been neglected, but it can be brought to life easily."

"I can't, now, my dear, but someday I'll go back."

Katya didn't ask any more questions. I escorted her to the railroad station and helped her carry her bundles. She had bought clothes for everyone. The bundles were heavy, and I strove with all my power not to lag behind her. That effort calmed my emotion.

"May God preserve you, Katerina."

"You too, Katya."

Thus we parted. I could have climbed onto the tram and taken it home, but for some reason I preferred to walk. The climb reminded me of Katya's kind face, and I clung to it for a moment as to an icon. It was hard for me to fall asleep that night. I saw the village and the meadows. Not for an instant did I forget that my parents hadn't loved me, that my aunts were harsh and wicked, but nevertheless I was stirred by longings for a plot of earth.

13

MY SECRET NOW DIVIDED US. Sometimes Sammy would turn to me, saying, "What are you thinking about?"

"Nothing."

We got up on time in the morning and went out to work. Usually, we would meet in the canteen at ten o'clock and drink a cup of coffee. That hour, despite the crowd, was an agreeable one for us. We were happy to be together. On the hard and unwelcoming benches of the canteen he told me several secrets about his past. I was afraid he would ask me a direct question.

Apparently, Sammy sensed my weakness and he allowed himself to stay longer at the tavern. He would return at ten o'clock, not drunk, just foggy, as though he knew I wouldn't scold him.

What would happen, and how would the days progress? I didn't know. Fear dominated me. To blunt the fear, I worked. I worked in the store and I worked at home, and sometimes I would get up early and prepare him a hot breakfast.

"Why all the bother?" He didn't understand.

"It's hard for me to sleep."

That was the absolute truth. As early as five, evil thoughts would crawl into my head and fill me with dread. I could, of course, have gone to a doctor secretly and had an abortion, but that thought frightened me even more. Village girls used to travel to the city to have abortions. Upon their return, their faces were dismayingly yellow.

"What are you thinking about?" he asked again.

"This and that."

"Something is disturbing you."

"Nothing at all."

The truth could no longer be concealed, but I, for some reason, did conceal it, as though burying my head in the sand.

Before we knew it, the long nights came, the sleepless nights. I felt ill, and I had to go outside and vomit. First he didn't notice, but when he did, the look of my body had already revealed the secret. Sammy opened his eyes and astonishment virtually froze them.

What could I say? I piled words upon words, and the more I added, the more his face froze. Before leaving for work, he said, "I'm very sorry. I don't know why I deserve this. There are things that are beyond my understanding." Each of his words, even the spaces between the words, cut into my flesh.

I was weak, but I still went to work. I didn't want to stay in the house. In the courtyard I saw Sammy. His back was bent, and he was busy sorting out the merchandise. I gathered my strength and approached. The frost in his eyes had not faded. The veins in the whites of his eyes now looked bulging and thick. His look wasn't hard, just weary.

"Forgive me," I said.

"No need to ask forgiveness."

"I don't know what to say."

He didn't answer. He walked away and immersed himself in his work. I stood where I was and watched his movements, constricted, like those of a man just now risen from his sickbed. In the evening, I served him a meal and he didn't say anything. I washed the dishes and did some laundry, and when I came back in, he had already fallen asleep.

Between us the words grew ever more limited. Jews don't beat you, but they get angry silently. I knew that. In the end I said, "I don't want to be a nuisance to you. As soon as the rains stop, I'll go back to my village. I have a house there."

Sammy fixed me with his icy gaze and said, "Don't talk nonsense." He made a convulsive gesture with his right hand, and that was the evil omen. He returned to the tavern and began drinking as in the past. First he would come home in a haze but not drunk. Before the week was out, he had ceased getting up to go to work. His face turned gray, and the tremor returned to his fingers. I was familiar with his drunkenness, and I wasn't afraid of it, but this time it turned out to be a different kind. He would return late, sit next to the table, and mutter in a mixture of Yiddish, German, and Ruthenian. In the past when he had gotten drunk, I used to entreat him, but now I stood at his side and kept silent. My silence only augmented the flow of his words. I wasn't afraid of him, only of his Ruthenian words.

Once I said to him, "Why don't you lie down and rest?"

"Don't tell me what to do!" he scolded.

He used to rise late and go to the tavern. That was how my father behaved in his time. For my part, I worked hard from morning to night, so that nothing would be lacking at home. What little love we had gradually disintegrated. Upon his return he would talk to me in Ruthenian, the way one talks to a despised servant.

"Sammy," I would plead with him.

"What are you talking about?" His eyes pushed me away.

One night he spoke to me, saying, "Why don't you bring me some vodka? I don't need either bread or potatoes."

"It's raining outside."

"I need a bottle of vodka right away." He eyes bulged and the blood in their veins poured out of them. This wasn't his normal anger. Ruthenian drunkenness had overpowered him. I wrapped myself in my coat and went out to fetch him a bottle. That night he sang and cursed the Jews and the Ruthenians. He didn't let me off easily, either. He called me a woman of the streets.

I was afraid and ran away.

Czernowitz is a big city. There's no end to its streets. I wandered without any destination. More than once I was about to go back, but I didn't have the strength to bear his eyes. His drunkenness wasn't violent, but the words he spat fell upon me like damp whips.

I would sleep in little Jewish-owned taverns. I had no choice but to sell another one of Henni's jewels. Every time I prepared to sell one, fear would possess me. The jewels were tied to my body, and it was hard for me to part with them.

This time the lot fell on a brooch made of thin strands of silver, with a large blue stone in the center. I touched it, and my fingers were scorched. I don't hate Jewish merchants, but I do hate jewelers. I sold them Henni's jewels for almost nothing. I was angry at them, but I wasn't angry at Sammy. If he had crossed my path, I would have gone to him. But Sammy didn't cross my path. I went from merchant to merchant and stood at their doors like a beggar. One of the merchants impudently asked me, "Where did you get the brooch if I may ask?"

"I didn't steal it, sir," I said, plucking up my courage.

Winter came, and I rented a room with a Jewish family. It was a poor family, burdened with many children, and the room was narrow, actually an alcove. Fortunately for me, it adjoined the apartment and absorbed some of its heat. I was glad to be in a Jewish house again, to hear the language, the prayers, and to divert myself with the thought that I had come home.

During these last days, I saw Rosa, and she had become very old. Her hair was thinned and gray, and one deep wrinkle divided the length of her face. For some reason I took it for the cut made by the murderer. Though the cut had healed, its depth was still visible. To my surprise there was no need to tell her anything. She knew everything and even pronounced Sammy's name. Every time I take the high road, I see Rosa. She's bound to my most secret thoughts. The last time, we spoke at length, and she was glad that I spoke the language fluently and pronounced the names of people and places correctly.

My landlady's name was Pearl, and she constantly marveled at my Yiddish. When I told her that Yiddish is a pleasing language, sweet to listen to, a suspicious smile crossed her lips. They kept the children away from me, and most of the day I was shut in my alcove, thinking and dozing off.

Selling the brooch was painful. The sum I got for it was large, and perhaps that's why I was able to block my tears. I paid my rent to the landlady. She couldn't believe her eyes, and in her embarrassment she told me, "You're good."

"What's good about it?" I asked.

"Everybody, until now, has cheated me, and you paid me on time."

Now, at night I sit on my bed and write down the events of the day. I acquired that habit from the time I dwelled with Rosa. My dear ones have left me, and now I have nothing in the world but my notes. I store all my thoughts in them. My notes are numerous and confused, and in some it's hard to make out the writing, but still I continue. I also write when I'm tired, because sometimes it seems to me that I must preserve every face and every detail, so that when the time comes I can go back and remember them. But in the meantime there was the fear. I was frightened of the winter silence, of the drunkards wandering in the streets, of policemen, of the mob of peasants sitting in wagons and playing dice. Fear lurked in all my limbs. I saw clearly that a tempest was brewing on the horizon and the mob would storm the Jewish houses. I remembered the sight of the young men of my village who would come home from looting, merry and drunk. I remembered my friend Waska, a quiet and decent lad. We used to herd the flocks together. I loved him because of his generosity, his manners, and his forthrightness. We used to spend many hours in the field, and after my father had married his second wife, I would stay with Waska till late at night. I preferred the darkness of night to my stepmother's face. That Waska, who used to hug and kiss me delicately, who was bashful about asking for my body, that darling Waska went out in the winter with all his friends to hunt Jews, and when a Jew who had crossed his path—not a young man—managed to slip out of his hands, Waska didn't give up. He ran after the Jew and caught him, venting all his fury. Not content, he dragged the Jew back to the village.

At Easter, the air of the village would be full of passion. The young men would unleash all their fury on the Jews. The reward wasn't slow in coming. If you captured a Jew, others would come to save him; if you caught a Jew, you were sure of getting a suitcase full of merchandise.

14

IN FEBRUARY, I gave birth to a son. The midwife, an old Jewish woman, informed me immediately that the child was sound in all his limbs and his weight was satisfactory. The labor was intense, but I was so excited I hadn't felt the pains.

The next day I told the landlady I wished to have the boy circumcised and would call him Benjamin. The landlady, a simple, loyal woman, who kept a stall where she sold candy and seeds, was shocked by my intention and said, "What are you thinking about? Why give the child a serious defect? He'll suffer from it all his life."

"I swore in my heart," I said.

"I don't understand you," she said.

I had abundant milk. I nursed the child morning, noon, and night. Strange, but for years I hadn't remembered the daughter born to me in Moldovitsa, and now, as I nursed Benjamin, I remembered her face with great clarity. For a moment a chill passed through my body. But the sadness proved to be a passing one. I was weary from giving birth, from nursing, and every time the baby fell asleep, I slept with him.

My thoughts grew narrower and narrower, and it's doubtful whether I was thinking at all.

"Where does the *mohel* live?" the words left my mouth.

"Why do you need him? Why?" The woman's open face bespoke honesty and loyalty.

"I'll pay him," I said in my great stupidity.

"He's a God-fearing man, and he wouldn't do something like that," said the woman, lowering her face.

The next day I went down to the train and traveled to a village. I guessed they wouldn't be as strict in the country. But I quickly discovered my error. I spent long hours in isolated taverns, struggling with all my power to get to a *mohel*. The people I met didn't encourage me. "What for?" they said. "One must protect oneself and one's children."

I had a long conversation with a widow in one of those narrow little roadside taverns. She spoke to me like a mother. "You're punishing your child with your own hands. Don't you see what they're doing to the Jews? Not a day passes without a murder, and you, instead of protecting him, want to give him a severe blemish. We have no choice, but you, with your own hands and a clear mind, you're sentencing him to a miserable fate." There was sharpness and honesty in her voice. But for some reason, I don't know where I found the strength, I repeated that single sentence like a fool. "I am determined to have the baby circumcised."

I roamed from village to village and from tavern to tavern. A few Jews lived in each village, and in every tavern I found quiet, marvelous people, who offered the baby a cup of warm milk and served me a mug of coffee, but they wouldn't heed my request, and more than once they reprimanded me. In my great anguish, I was about to open my mouth and tell them: I'm a Ruthenian, the daughter of Ruthenians, but my fate has pulled me from my ancestors, and now I have nothing to grasp except the hems of Jewish homes. In my heart I knew no one would understand, so I kept silent. Finally, in one isolated village I found a Jewish grocer who served as an occasional *mohel*. He saw my distress and agreed to circumcise my son. His agreement astonished me, and I burst into tears.

That night I didn't sleep. Evil thoughts tormented me, and as though to bring my dread to a boil, the baby was relaxed and suckled quietly. The thought that the next morning he would be circumcised suddenly cast fear upon me, and I wanted to flee the place. But my resolution was stronger than my fear, and I didn't budge from the house.

Early in the morning they circumcised him, and I couldn't restrain myself. I sobbed like a servant woman. When I was aroused from my faint and saw that the child was breathing, I felt easier. I took the landlady's hands, bowed down, and kissed her, as we do in the village.

The first night after the circumcision I didn't sleep. The baby, to my surprise, didn't cry but only murmured and sighed. I stood next to his wretched little cradle, and my mouth emitted words I had likely heard in my childhood in the meadows.

For a month I stayed in the *mohel*'s house. His wife prepared me milk porridge and a cup of coffee every morning. I nursed the boy day and night. A kind of oblivion, such as I had not known all my life, enfolded me, and I slept for many hours. Again I was in Henni's company. Henni told me many things about her childhood and about her parents, who pinched pennies so she could study with a famous teacher. The teacher's demands were many and difficult. After a day of torture, she would return home by the night train. More than once she begged: Let me be; I don't want to be a pianist. But her parents didn't listen. If she refused to rise in the morning, they made her get up, and if she refused to take the train, one of her parents, usually the mother, would escort her. Thus for years and years. When she was twenty, she ran away from home with Izio. Her mother, greatly upset, returned to her faith and began to take fastidious pains at home and with her husband.

"It's good you've got a baby," said Henni. "If I had had a baby, I wouldn't have committed suicide. But why did you have him circumcised?"

"That's what my heart told me to do."

"The Jews have no particular excellence—the same stupidity and the same wickedness."

"What can I do? I only feel at peace among Jews."

My answer saddened her, and she curled up, folding her legs as she used to do in life. A hard sadness and total self-abnegation.

"You're angry at me." I couldn't contain myself.

"I'm astounded at your hard-heartedness."

"Why do you say hard-heartedness?"

"What else can I call it? Do you have another word? A person takes a healthy child and gives it a scar. What can we say? What can we call that crime?"

I wanted to cry, but my tears welled up within me, and I didn't utter a word.

I opened my eyes, and I was afraid to stay in the house

any longer. Henni's appearance had horrified me. There and then, I decided to set out. "Why won't you stay longer? It's cold out," the landlady pleaded.

"I must be on my way," I said without explanation.

The snow was silent and a cold sun glittered in the sky. I wrapped up Benjamin and paid the sum we had agreed upon. The woman, to my surprise, wasn't satisfied and asked for more. I added more, but I couldn't seal my lips, and I said, "Why did you do that?"

"I demanded what was coming to us, no more."

"Hadn't we agreed on a price?"

"We did everything required—and more," the woman replied in frightfully businesslike tones.

Not until I was outdoors, in the cold sun, did I feel what my days in the *mohel*'s house had done to me. In my heart I regretted that we had parted that way. There's no touch in this world that doesn't leave a scratch. I wanted to go back and ask forgiveness, but for some reason I didn't. Now, when I picture that woman, I know she wasn't evil or miserly, just bitter. Her barrenness cried out from within her.

I stood at the village square and didn't know which way to turn. Without Henni's jewels, who knows where I would have ended up. I bundled Benjamin in two fur wraps, and he slept quietly. His tranquil sleep strengthened me, and I was willing to set out on foot.

"Where are you going?" An old peasant stopped his wagon.

I told him the name of the nearby village.

"Get up."

"How much must I pay?"

"Nothing at all."

After an hour's ride, he asked, "Where are you from?"
I told him.

"But you don't look like someone from a village."

"Then from where?"

"I don't know."

"From the village, father, from the meadow." The old melody of my mother tongue rose within me.

"There's something in your voice."

"What, father?"

"Some other tune."

"I don't understand."

"And what were you doing here?" he probed.

"I was visiting relatives," I lied.

"I wouldn't let my daughter go out on a trip alone."

"Why?"

"The road spoils you. A person soaks up foreign terms, foreign gestures. We Ruthenians must watch ourselves. Jews ruin everything. Now they're spoiling our women. You mustn't work for the Jews. The Jews corrupt one's soul."

I got down at the next village square and was glad to be free of that man and his reproaches.

15

THE SNOW MELTED, and a bright sun hung in the sky. I regretted the incident with the *mohel*'s wife. Had it not been for that scratch, I would bear her face with love. Now the memory was stained, and I will remember only her last look. That aftertaste did not cloud my spirit for long. I immediately saw that I was in a Jewish street full of good smells.

It turned out that Passover was coming. Anyone who has ever been in a Jewish home at Passover will never forget it. The ceremony lasts about three weeks—about two weeks of preparations, the holiday itself, and the end. The stages are clear, without any superfluity. I was with Rosa only a few years, but still the holidays are stamped into my flesh like fire. Now the air is purged of all odor; its cleanliness chokes me. Now there are no Jews in the world, and I'm the only one, in secret, evoking the memory of their holidays in my notebook. Were it not for the world to come, there would be no purpose in my old life.

I've put the cart before the horse. I was in Zhadova on

market day, and everybody was gathered in the square. Toward Passover, everyone whitewashed the outer walls of their homes. The low houses, which were steeped in mud all winter, now rose from their humble position, standing straight and sparkling in light blue. "From the depths, I cried to you, O Lord," we read in the Book of Books. Anyone who has ever seen the low houses rising out of the mudbanks understands that verse literally.

While I was still riveted to the spot, the old urge overcame me. For more than two months I hadn't had a drink. I sipped two drinks and came right out, so that Benjamin wouldn't get used to those odors or to the language of the peasants. In the tavern, people do what they please. There, nothing is permitted or forbidden. I swore in my soul that for Benjamin's sake, I would keep my distance from taverns. I wanted to raise him in quiet, clean surroundings. Benjamin's face was open, and a great light canopied his eyes. When he opened his big, bright eyes, a smile would break out between his lips. Three times a day I used to nurse him, and those few hours of closeness were my joy.

I rented a room from a Jewish family. The Jews are very strict on Passover, yet it's not a panicked strictness but an attentive caution, like a gradual purification.

I paid the rent in advance and received an attic room. My status in that area was strange. The Ruthenians scented out that something had gone wrong in me. The look of my face, though, hadn't changed, but a few movements, perhaps a few accents in my speech, had become warped. With the Jews, my status was clearer: I was a servant in a Jewish house, spoke a good Yiddish, was familiar with the practices and customs, and they had to be careful in front of me. A Jew is a cautious creature, and he's especially cautious with servant women who have worked in Jewish homes.

"How many years did you work for the Jews?" The landlady interrogated me.

"Many years."

"With observant people?"

"Also with observant people."

"And why don't you go back to your village?"

I was used to these questions. Every servant woman is suspect of thievery, of tale-bearing. In her presence one doesn't speak openly. But what is there to do? I also understand that secret language, and that amuses me. More than once I wanted to reveal it to them: I understand every word, every remark, and every hint. You have nothing to fear; I won't steal and I won't inform on you. I only want refuge at night.

Now it seemed to me that they regretted renting me the attic. I seldom went downstairs, only once or twice a day, no more. The landlord never ceased reproaching his wife for renting the attic. "Where will I have a place to myself during the holiday? Where can I open a book? Every corner is taken. It won't be easy to get that stranger out of the house."

"What can I do?" the woman apologized. "She paid me in advance. A nice sum, you can't deny." The landlord wasn't appeased. He exacted a promise from her that she would never rent out the attic again.

But in the meanwhile I had a broad view from the window. In the center were many Jewish houses, low, small shops, among them a tailor's and a cobbler's. On rainy days the light in the sky was extinguished, and the place looked like a gray, flat swamp, but on days when the sun shone, the place sprang to life and all the preparations were in full swing.

I was glad to have Benjamin with me in that hubbub. I remember clearly how my beloved Benjamin used to gather up the last remains of leavened bread on the eve before the holiday and utter his blessings by candlelight. The actual burning of the leavened bread took place the next day. That burning involved no particular ceremony, but to me it seemed as though a great secret was hidden in that small activity.

The landlord never stopped grumbling. "Why did you let a stranger into the house just before Passover? I saw her wandering around the kitchen. I don't know how I can lead the Seder. It's not enough for me that there are *goyim* outside. Now they're in my house." The landlady didn't respond to him any longer. Finally, she said, "What can I do? I made a mistake."

Those clear voices were hard on me. But I didn't take offense. I knew the Jews well. All year long they lived a hard, scattered life. On his holiday a Jew wanted to be by himself and with his book. In order to diminish my presence, right after nursing, I went down to the streets of the village. Every day the preparations for the holiday intensified. Only among the Jews is there that anxiety. Seen from a certain distance away from the market, they looked like tiny workers passing tiny bricks from hand to hand and bringing them rapidly to the scaffolding, where the bricks were carried up to build a great wall. Only on the very last day before the holiday did the bustle recede, and a kind of calm suddenly fell on the streets and muted them.

The holiday came. I opened the door of the attic so that Benjamin could absorb the story of the Exodus from Egypt in its entirety. A baby learns in its mother's womb, and even more so outside it. It was important for him to soak up those melodies while he was still an infant. I remember my beloved Benjamin conducting the Seder. It was a Seder without any formalities or grand gestures. Now too I identified the sounds, and I knew: They're dividing the matzoh, dipping, eating parsley and bitter herb, and I was happy that Benjamin was absorbing those sounds unobstructed. When the day came, though I would no longer be in this world, he would remember and say: Almighty God, where did I hear those voices? They're familiar to me.

Benjamin was developing, and he looked like a six-month-old baby. I spoke to him a lot and explained to him that this was his second stop. The first was with the *mohel*, who had removed his foreskin and hurt him. Now it was Passover, the time of our freedom, and it was important to hear the melodies of freedom that were filling the house. I told him about little Moses, whom they hid from the murderers in a basket. For many days he drifted on the great river, and when he grew up he became a savior, because he saw with his own eyes how great was the travail and how hard the servitude.

The intermediate days of Passover were half holidays. People stood in the street and conversed. There was no haste. Sometimes it seemed to me that it wasn't a holiday but rather a kind of excitement. The Jewish holiday, especially Passover, echoed over a distance. Every holiday painted the sky with its colors. Passover, for example, was bright blue. I wanted to tell that to Benjamin, but Benjamin didn't listen to me. He was completely immersed in suckling. He nursed hard and weakened me. But I overcame my weakness.

The days were warm now, and the windows of the houses were opened wide. I too went out to the grass, spread a blanket, and put Benjamin down on it. Benjamin had gotten plump, I found. His eyes were wide open and lively, and he followed every sound. But as for me, my spirit was clouded. I no longer saw my dear ones in my dreams at night. My sleep was deep but opaque, as though I lay at the bottom of a pit. Where are you, my dears? I groped, and I awakened soaked with sweat. Most of the day I was outdoors. I kept away from the taverns so as not to be tempted. There were many taverns in this little village, mostly belonging to Jews. During the holiday and the intermediate days, the odor of vodka wasn't perceptible, but now it wafted into every corner, arousing desire in me.

The landlady wasn't talkative; her face was turned inward, and when I asked her something, she answered with the utmost brevity. At night I woke from a nightmare: a Ruthenian thug had tried to snatch Benjamin from my arms. He looked like one of my cousins. I struggled with him with all my strength, and when I couldn't overcome him, I sank my teeth into him. He let go and cleared out. That bad dream left its mark on me. The next day I felt very weak. My fingers were frozen. I did go down to the grass, but I didn't let Benjamin play on the blanket. I held him in both hands. That evening I heard the landlord ask his wife, "When is she going to leave us?"

"In two weeks."

"It's hard for me to bear her."

"She doesn't do anything. She's quiet."

"I need that attic like air to breathe. Why did you do that to me?"

"We didn't have any cash, don't you remember?"

"For cash you deprive me of my corner?"

"Excuse me," said the woman in a choked voice.

The next day I got up early, packed up my few belongings, wrapped up Benjamin, and announced that I was leaving the house.

16

I HEADED NORTH. It was easy to travel in that season. The roads were full of wagons and carriages. You got up on a wagon, and no one asked you where you were headed. At night we used to sleep in little inns, tucked away out of sight, deep within the hilltops.

After my nightmare, fear didn't loosen its grip on me. It sometimes felt as if my entire village was chasing me. I knew it was only vain imagining, an impression, restlessness, but it was hard for me to dislodge the fear. I ran from place to place, and every morning I blessed my life and my son's life.

Just a year ago I had had strong bonds with Rosa and with Henni. I spoke to them face to face, without barriers. Now my sleep was thick and dreamless. I woke up in panic and started to pack my belongings.

"Where are you hurrying to?" a familiar voice suddenly asked me in clear Yiddish.

"I have to get to Czernowitz," I answered for some reason.

"But drink something first. Give the boy something to

drink. In this season there are wagons, and if fortune smiles on you, you'll even find a coach."

Her voice was like the essence of silence. Only a believer has such a quiet voice. She prepared porridge for the baby and a mug of coffee for me. The old woman's soft movements calmed me, and I wanted to weep. Benjamin clung to me and smiled.

"Where are you from, my dear?" she asked.

"I'm a gentile." I didn't conceal it.

"I see," said the old woman. "But you've soaked up a lot of Jewishness."

"For years I worked in the home of an observant Jew."

"But your voice tells me that you were always close to the Jews."

"Since my youth."

"And now what do you want to do?"

"I want to raise my son, Benjamin, in a clean, quiet house. I want to keep him away from coarse voices and from crudeness. I want him to see a lot of trees and a lot of water, and I don't want him to be in the company of horsemen."

The old woman looked at me with her good eyes and said, "It's been a long time since I heard a voice like yours. Who was that woman you worked for in your youth?"

I told her.

"And where is that woman?"

"She was murdered by thugs, she and her late husband."

"They don't give us any peace, my dear. Here too the murderers' hands are full of blood. My son-in-law, may he rest in peace, was murdered ten years ago, in this courtyard. He was sitting on a bench and drinking a cup of coffee, and suddenly the murderer came and struck him with an ax."

"And you aren't afraid to live here, mother?"

"I rise every morning and deliver my life and all my wishes into God's hands. Let Him do with them as He desires. Once I was very frightened of death. Now I am no longer frightened. I have many dear ones in the world of truth. I won't be alone there."

The village Jews were creatures of a special kind. The trees and the silence purified their faith. They spoke about matters great and small with the same simplicity. The peasants admired them, were afraid of them, and when their bigotry welled up, they murdered them.

"The Jews should leave the village. The village is a trap," I said.

"You're right, my dear. But I'll never leave here. Here I was born and here, apparently, will be my grave."

I paid her for the night's lodging and added a few pennies.

"You added too much. A person must save his money for times of trouble," she said.

I looked at her face and said to myself, A person doesn't meet a countenance like this every day. People are stingy and mean as if this world were an eternity. I shall preserve her face in my heart. That day, her face told me that death is not the end.

The sun was full, and I walked on foot. I was happy with Benjamin, and happy among the trees. When I got tired, I would spread a blanket on the earth and offer him whatever was in my bag: cheese, soft bread, a tomato, a mashed egg. He ate everything that came to hand. There was no need to feed him. And when he was happy, he rolled on the grass like a puppy, laughing and voicing little bleats like a baby kid.

But the nights frightened me. I tried to overcome fear, but fear was stronger. Sometimes Benjamin also woke from a dream and scared me. I told him that dreams are meaningless: Your mother's at your side; she'll always be at your side. There's nothing to be afraid of. I hugged him hard, and he calmed down.

In the morning Benjamin spoke his first word. He said, "Mommy," and he said it in Yiddish. He immediately laughed out loud.

"Say it again."

He laughed and said it again.

Now it was clear to me that Yiddish would be his language. That discovery made me happy. The thought that my son would talk Rosa's and Benjamin's language seemed to fill my heart with new hope, but why did my hands tremble?

The next day I taught him a new word: *hand*. I showed him my hand, and he said, "Hand." He rolled on the grass with the words, repeating them with the sweet accent of a baby, bringing tears to my eyes. The green meadows extended as far as the horizon and evoked in me, against my will, the meadows of my native village. Now they seemed so far away to me, as if they had never existed.

So we went on. Every night in a different inn. The proprietors of the inns didn't always smile upon us. It was fortunate that I could pay for a hot meal. After a day of walking, the two of us were bone weary. Benjamin spoke a few words of Yiddish, and everybody laughed.

"Where did he learn?" asked the Jewish owner of an inn.

"From me."

"What does he need that for?"

"So he won't be a goy."

I knew that answer would make him laugh, and he did laugh indeed.

It was very hard for me to do without a drink. I promised myself not to drink, and I kept my promise, but I paid in blood. At night I woke up short of breath, my hands trembling. It was a hideous torture, and sometimes I asked myself if it wouldn't be better to have a drink. After all, it was no sin.

I shall never forget that summer. But the autumn abruptly came and cut off my happiness. It was a muddy autumn, flooded with wild rains, which would suddenly slash down and drown the roads in mire, and we would be in a neglected inn, among toughs and drunkards, the floor full of filth and the bed not clean.

"Where's the kid from?"

"He's mine."

"Why does he talk Yiddish?"

"He doesn't talk. He just babbles." I tried to shield him.

"You should be ashamed of yourself."

"Why?"

"Take him to a village quickly so that he'll learn a human language. Even a Ruthenian bastard is a Ruthenian. Only children of the devil talk Yiddish."

"He's not a bastard."

"What is he then? Was he born with a priest's blessing?"

"He's mine."

To my misfortune, Benjamin began to recite all the words I'd taught him. I tried to shush him, but I didn't succeed.

He laughed and babbled, and every word that came out of his mouth was clear and distinct. It was impossible to mistake them; the child was talking Yiddish.

"Get him out of here," shouted one of the drunkards.

"Where can I take him?"

"Take him outside."

I was depressed and had a few drinks. The drinks warmed me and imbued me with courage. Fear left me, and I informed them clearly, leaving no possibility for misunderstanding, that I had no intention of returning to my village, no matter what. The village was full of coarseness and wickedness, and not even the beasts of the field were innocent there.

"Servant girl," one of them cursed at me.

"Villain," I didn't hold my tongue.

"Whore!" he said, and spat.

I left the inn and found refuge in a barn. I blocked the window with two big bales of hay, wrapped up Benjamin, and clutched him tightly to my body. After an hour of shivering, he fell asleep in my arms.

17

WINTER CAME ALL AT ONCE, and strongly. The inns were empty and cold, and the landlords were irritable. Benjamin cried, and I was helpless. The winter winds now prevailed over the area. I stood next to the windows, which were coated with frost, stamping my feet in great desperation.

I was willing to pay any price to heat the room, but the landlord was stingy about every piece of wood, stubbornly repeating the same argument: One must save. Who knows what frost we could expect this winter. Just a few days ago the roads were full of people, wagons, coaches galloping in every direction, and now there was no memory of them, only winds and snow.

One of the wagon drivers agreed to take me to the railroad station, but in the end he changed his mind.

"I'm willing to take the chance," I told him.

"A mother with a tender babe mustn't take risks," he reproached me.

He was afraid, and he had reason to be afraid: The

storms raged and plucked at the roofs of the houses.

Finally, I had no alternative but to threaten the proprietor of the inn. If he didn't give me wood, I would summon the police. That threat made an impression. Immediately, he let me take wood from the storeroom.

"We thought you were softer," said the landlord.

"Why?"

"You speak fine Yiddish."

"So for that we have to freeze?"

"I understand," said the proprietor of the inn, without explaining himself.

Imperceptibly, the winter, which assailed me and confined me in that miserable inn, aroused my old, dormant vitality. I was talking the way they talk in the village, without ceremony. Let people know that the world isn't lawless. Benjamin also mustn't be soft. A weak Jew arouses dark instincts.

"You must be strong," I drill into Benjamin. He laughs, and his laugh has the sound of glass bells. If you are strong, your mother will be strong too. Indeed, Benjamin gained strength from day to day. His hands gripped me powerfully. And when he got angry, he scratched. The scratches hurt me, but I was pleased by his anger. After he scratched, he crawled under the table, hiding and laughing.

I trained Benjamin to stand. Standing demanded a great effort from him, but he triumphed and stood steady. I had no doubt that he would be muscular and sturdy. His vocabulary also grew from day to day. Now he made a lot of sounds. To make him laugh I would whisper a word in Ruthenian to him. He would laugh as though I had uttered absolute nonsense.

Outside, there was no change. Snow was heaped up on top of snow. I had no need of luxuries. I bought provisions from the landlady and cooked modest meals. Benjamin ate everything and had a healthy appetite. In the evening, he dropped to the floor and fell asleep. His ability to fall asleep was astonishing. He fell asleep instantly. From him I learned that the line between wakefulness and sleep is very thin. My sleep wasn't tranquil. Visions invaded me from all sides and made me dizzy. The landlord raised the price of firewood again. He claimed that the market price had gone sky high. I paid him without a murmur. I had a hunch he was prof-iteering. The landlord knew that now I couldn't leave, so he could take advantage of me. I paid him. Later I didn't keep silence, and I told him: "You mustn't profiteer. The Jews received the Torah, and they must observe it." The landlord was surprised by my argument. He spread out his bills and receipts before me and showed me that he wasn't profiteering. On the contrary, his losses were great. I didn't believe him, and I told him that I didn't believe him. That winter my hunches got stronger, and I wasn't afraid to express them.

"You're embittering my life." He appealed to my con-science.

Benjamin had changed me. I became slightly plump, but my movements weren't confined. I crawled with him under the table, jumped rope, and rolled the length of the room with him.

The members of the household were wary with me, sel-dom speaking in my presence and then weighing every word before it was uttered. They were afraid I would inform on them. I had no intention of informing. Tale-bearing is a contemptible trait. Only the basest people are informers. I wanted to tell them that, but I knew that my words would only increase their suspicion. I remembered: Scoundrels had informed on Rosa, and Rosa had had to run from office to office to disprove the false accusation. When she came home, she would fall on the floor and weep in great sorrow and shame. I wouldn't inform, because the Torah commanded us not to spread gossip, I thought of telling them, but immediately changed my mind, lest it sound self-righteous.

In a short time, when we got to Czernowitz, I would read to Benjamin from books. Benjamin would open his big eyes and listen. That thought, for some reason, moved me greatly. Now every little movement of Benjamin's brought me to tears. I must be strong, I told myself, and I stifled my tears.

The next day the storm died down, and a bright winter sky was revealed in its full splendor. I must set out, I said, as though a home were waiting for me in the distance. During the past weeks I had found that my presence was very burdensome to the landlord. Every time I appeared in the corridor, the landlady drew back. The landlord didn't show himself very much, either. He ignored me. My room was very close to their bedroom, and they didn't allow themselves a single superfluous word. Don't talk, I heard the landlord's voice.

I packed up my few belongings, wrapped Benjamin in furs, and paid. The landlord didn't ask for anything extra, and he didn't say thank you. No one was in the hall of the inn at that time, and I set out without a blessing.

The bright sun didn't lessen the cold. The chill was fierce, but I knew I had to leave that place behind and move on.

"Climb in." A peasant stopped his sled.

"Where to?"

"Czernowitz."

"How did you know?"

"I guessed."

Thus he decided instead of me. He was an old peasant, transporting a few crates of apples, some bundles of dry fruit, and a box of fresh dairy products in his sled. In the front corner he had left a vacant spot for a passenger.

"I don't like riding alone," he confided.

"How long will we be traveling?"

"Till evening."

Benjamin fell asleep in my arms. Only now did I notice how much he had grown during the winter months. His face had filled out and golden hair covered his forehead; the folds in his cheeks had melted, and a new layer of pink padded them.

"Where do you live?"

"In the city," I stated flatly, without furnishing details.

"But you're from the country, right?"

"Correct, uncle." I used village language.

"You work for Jews?"

"Correct, uncle."

The trip was fast and even, and in the afternoon we stopped at a tavern. I had a very strong urge to go up to the bar and order a drink, but I controlled myself. I stayed in my seat and watched over Benjamin's sleep. It was a Ruthenian tavern, the kind that gave off the stink of manure and vodka day and night, and which one didn't leave till one had inebriated each and every limb in one's body.

When the peasant returned to his sled, he scolded me for not coming in and sharing a drink. A person without a drink isn't a person. Drink arouses the body and allows a person to speak openly.

18

I HAD A PRECIOUS TREASURE, a great treasure. I looked in his eyes, and I couldn't believe my own. He was all light. We lived in a one-room apartment on the Jews' street. It was April already, but the frosty wind still blew strongly. I stood at the window with Benjamin for hours, and thanks to his large eyes, I too saw miracles.

"Bird, Mama."

"Bird."

"All gone bird. All gone bird."

Every word that left his mouth was like a joyous trumpet sounding.

Once again the nights hummed with quiet joy. I entertained my dear ones in my home, Rosa and Benjamin, and sometimes Henni too. My Benjamin spoke astonishingly well. Everyone called him the little prodigy, and I was astonished that I hadn't heard that word before, a pretty word. Suddenly, Sammy broke in again, very drunk. I tried to hide him from my guests, but he overcame me, broke into the center of the room, and announced that the tyke was no miracle, just an unwanted child.

"You must watch over him carefully," Rosa warned me.

"I'll guard him like the apple of my eye," I promised.

"He's a marvelous child."

Passover was again approaching, and I stood at the window so that he could see the movement, absorb the odors, and know that every holiday has its own color. The world isn't confusion the way it sometimes seems. If Rosa were with us, we would celebrate the Seder with her. My dear ones were snatched away from me before their time. Had it not been for Henni, who removed me from the sewers of the railroad station, I would be wallowing there to this day.

Every few months, I sold a piece of jewelry. Every jewel I sold ripped my body. But the thought that I was raising a child, and that he would brighten everyone's eyes, slightly sweetened my sadness. The jewels lay on my breast.

The thought that I had my own room and that my son was standing at the window and looking—those thoughts gladdened me always. In the evening I used to dress Benjamin, and we would go out to listen to the night noises. There were evil creatures in the city: drunkards who remembered me from the station, people from my village who lurked in wait for me, and plain evildoers who accosted me. I wasn't afraid. When Benjamin was in my arms, I wasn't afraid. Step aside and don't stand in my way, I used to warn them, and if they provoked me, I cursed them and the mother who bore them.

One evening someone from my own village accosted me. He knew me at first glance and wouldn't let up. I implored him, "We both grew up in the same godforsaken hole, my father knew yours, why are you annoying me?"

"Put down the bastard and come with me." He didn't heed my pleas.

"Why are you calling my son a bastard?" I couldn't keep back my voice.

"Because he's a bastard."

I implored him, You see that I'm a woman alone, bringing up a child on my own. It isn't easy to raise a child. But I'm doing it gladly, because he's a good child. I spoke to him the way you talk to a relative, with all the homey words I had, but he stood his ground.

"Put down the bastard. I have a room not far from here."

"How are you talking to a mother? I'm not a young girl anymore."

"You sleep with everyone, but you won't sleep with me."

"Don't talk down to me."

"I need to sleep with a woman tonight," he said to me with a bestial voice.

"Take some other woman. There are lots of women. Why do you want a woman with a child?"

"I feel like sleeping with you."

I mustered my strength and raised my voice, saying to him, "If you get close to me, I'll bite you like a bitch."

"Whore," he hissed.

"Bastard." I wasn't mute.

I was glad I had fought for my life. That night we didn't stroll around anymore. We went back home while it was still light, and I immediately said to Benjamin, "You must be a brave boy. Without courage, there's no life. We must exercise every morning. You have to make your muscles firm and be a lion cub." I myself learned courage the old way. I had two or three drinks, my body warmed up, and I saw my departed mother before my eyes. My mother was a brave woman. Everyone was afraid of her. She never drank in public, always by herself, mainly at night.

In the evening, when we went out for a walk, I told Benjamin, "Don't be afraid. When a person overcomes fear, he's free. Fear makes everything ugly. You have to walk erect." I doubted whether he understood, but I recited that lesson so that when the time came, when he needed it, it would be ready in his mind.

Nevertheless, our walks weren't tranquil any longer. The city was full of peasants and peddlers, everybody shouting, threatening, and cursing one another. The sight wasn't a pretty one. Except for the old Jews who would stand by the doors of their meager shops at that hour. Were it not for those thin creatures, who always spread awe, I would have shut myself inside my room. I was bound up with the gazes of those old men, sometimes forgetting that the city was swarming with evildoers.

Sometimes a man accosted me, and I would escape from him into a tavern. In the tavern, I would often meet my old acquaintances. I had met many people in my life. They wanted my body, and I had usually given them what they wanted.

"How are you, Katerina?" one of them called. They'd gotten older, too. Vodka had emptied their faces, and the skin of their hands had yellowed. Nevertheless, they asked, "Where can we find you, Katerina?"

"I've come home," I said.

"What's the matter? Has some disaster happened?"

"A person has to go home, isn't that right?" I answered them in the language of the village.

That excuse was acceptable to them, for some reason, and they let me be.

But that one bully, that revolting villager, didn't forget me, and every day he lay in wait for me. I sensed he was lurking, but because I didn't see him, I believed it was just fear. During the last few days I stopped walking in side streets. We stayed in the center of town and went home early. I sensed that the hyena was lying in wait for me. At home I wasn't tranquil, either. Every noise alarmed me, but I still refused to bolt the door. You mustn't fear, I repeated to myself. If I'm afraid, Benjamin will be afraid too.

On Passover eve I was very happy, and in my great joy I swung Benjamin up in the air. Benjamin laughed, and his laughter rang out in the street. Afterward, I bought him some ice cream, and he asked for another portion. I bought it for him and called him my little glutton. He laughed. A few peasants stood at the side of the street, and they laughed too. No one disturbed me. Everyone was busy with final preparations for the holiday, and I, in my great haste, with a kind of recklessness, turned into an alley that would shorten my path home.

Just as I stepped in, as though out of a pit, that thug emerged and barred my way. I knew that was my end, but I still shouted, "Don't touch me." It was the same brute, that Karil, that villain, who had harassed me a few days earlier, but now there was courage in his eyes. He was inebriated but not drunk.

"Put down the bastard and come with me." He grabbed my arm.

"I'm not afraid. You can slaughter me."

"I said what I said, and I won't go back on it."

"I'm afraid only of God."

"Put down the bastard," he said, baring his teeth.

Murderer, I was about to shout, but before my voice could manage, he grabbed Benjamin from my arms and smashed his body against the wall. I saw, God in heaven, the divine head of my son, that vessel more precious than all vessels, smashed in two and spatters of blood darkening the dusk. For a moment I froze, but immediately, swiftly, I took out my jackknife. I leaped forward and grabbed his neck and cut and cut. I felt the knife in the tendons of his flesh and my hands dripping with blood. The thug flopped under my hands, he kicked his feet, but I didn't let up. I carved him the way they butcher a beast in a meat shop.

19

THAT WAS HALF MY LIFE. From now on the color of my life is red. I too was murdered that evening. What remains of me is a stump. Two men dragged me along the streets the way one drags a long sack. "Murderess, murderess." I heard the voices slipping over my body like ice. Afterward, I didn't hear, only echoes that shattered with deafening noise. As they dragged it, my body lost its weight and the pain froze.

For a long time they dragged me, and I was sure that it was my end, but I wasn't afraid. Relief, the kind one feels after six or seven glasses of vodka, enveloped me. If this is death, it isn't so dreadful, I told myself. Eventually, the men dragging me got tired and left me on the pavement, but they didn't stop proclaiming, "Murderess, murderess." People crowded in from all around. In the turmoil I remembered that the Slavo brothers had cried out a similar shout after they had hunted down the wolf that had eaten their younger brother and brought it to the village square.

"Whom did she murder?" asked a man with a young voice.

"She murdered and carved him up."

"Where are you taking her?"

"To the police."

The questions and answers were so clear, as though they had passed through a fine sieve. I opened my eyes and saw a mass of people surrounding me in a black circle. The men who'd dragged me stood near me and panted heavily. I knew that if they only gave their assent, the mob would trample me.

The pause didn't last long. Now they dragged me with renewed strength, as though trying to dislocate my arms. And I felt how my body was borne, pounded and carried up as in a storm, as though they were afraid I might die before it was determined who was the monster in their hands.

The police building turned out to be close by. "A murderess," they said, and left me.

"Whom did she murder?"

"She carved him into pieces. Everything is lying in the street."

Apparently, I fainted or fell into a heavy sleep. When I woke I felt that the blood on my hands had coagulated. No memory was within me, like a bucket that has been emptied.

"She won't talk." I heard a man's voice.

"Did you beat her?"

"I beat her."

I felt no pain. The thought that they had beaten me and I didn't feel the blows roused me from my faint. In the next room, which was lit, voices rustled, but to my ears they sounded as though they came from a distance.

At night I was awake and I pressed myself against the

wall. The wall was cold and moldy, and I felt the cold trickling through my pores. My coat was torn, but the lining was intact. I straightened my legs, and then I saw for the first time that my knee was swollen. The swelling was huge and painful. That means, I said to myself, it's bad swelling. In the next room the voices didn't cease. First it seemed that they were talking about me, but it soon became clear that they were talking about some old mortgage. One of the voices complained that his mortgage was making a pauper of him. If it weren't for the mortgage, he'd be a free man.

It was as if my memory plunged deep within me, but I took in the motions and grating noises that happened around me very well. And I also noticed that the bars of the cell were thick but not close together.

I managed to take off my shoes. My ankles also proved to be swollen, but not excessively. I remembered that my mother used to say, "Katerina tears her socks so that they can't be darned anymore. I've already gotten tired of telling her that she's not allowed to crawl on the floor." I was three then, my father and mother still talked to each other, and my mother, for some reason, complained about me, a fond complaint, and I was glad that my mother loved me.

Later, a policeman approached and stood at the door of the cell. He seemed gigantic. He looked at me the way one looks at an unruly cow and ordered, "Get up, murderess." Hearing his voice, I got up on all fours, but it wasn't in my power to rise. He saw clearly that I was trying to get up, but my efforts seemed insufficient, and he beat me with his club. The blow was strong and knocked me over.

"What do you want from me?" I said.

"Don't talk to me like a human."

"What am I supposed to do?"

"Don't play the innocent. Talk like a murderess, understand?"

Then two men came and hoisted me up and put me in a lighted room. The sight of my face was, apparently, horrifying. They stood at a distance from me and spoke in Romanian. I didn't understand a word. One of the policemen addressed me in Ruthenian, asking, "Why did you kill him?" I don't remember what I answered. They, apparently, slapped my face and kicked me. I fell, and they kept kicking me. I didn't scream, and that drove them mad. In the end they brought me back to the cell. I don't know how many days I was kept away from the light of day. The darkness in the cell was great. All that time I felt that I was being swept away in a broad, deep river. Black waves covered me, but I, with a fish's gills, overcame the drowning. When I managed to open my eyes, I saw it was the Prut River; its flow heavy and red.

20

I WAS TRANSFERRED TO the prison on Sunday. Bells rang, and an autumn sun flooded the streets. Two armed gendarmes led me, and from every side people pointed: the monster. I was empty and frozen, and no pain annoyed me. In fact, it seemed to me that at that pace, I could march for hours. For the first time I felt my mother within me, not the mother who used to beat me but the courageous mother, who had wanted to teach me courage all those years and didn't know how. Now I strode with her, indivisible, like a single body.

Thus my new life began. The women in the prison knew everything, all the details, and they didn't greet me. In time I learned that they didn't greet other women with joy, either. A person who enters prison knows that here one doesn't die, one falls apart. No thread will mend the tears. It wasn't the walls that frightened me but the faces.

The trial had not been long. I admitted every detail of the accusation, and the old judge said that he had not met with such a horror to that day. If it hadn't been the murder of a murderer, he would have ordered that my neck be placed in a hangman's noose. There was no one in the courtroom. The defense attorney appointed by the court told me, "You can be content. As long as there's life, there's hope." He was a Jewish lawyer, who scurried from place to place and seemed embarrassed by himself. He reminded me of Sammy for some reason, though there was no resemblance between them.

Life in prison was very orderly. We rose early and lights-out was at eight-thirty. Between rising and going to sleep —labor. One squad went to work outside in a textile factory, another worked in the field, and another maintained the prison. Once the legs of the women prisoners had been chained, but that practice had been abolished. Later they were tied together by a rope and led in groups of three. Each squad numbered thirty women. Some old women bore their punishment with contempt and a straight back. At the age of seventy, the prisoners were freed for life, but not always. There was one ninety-year-old woman in the prison.

I was attached to the maintenance squad. I was alert and did what I was supposed to, but my life was narrow, like that of a beast of burden. After ten hours of scouring floors, I would sink onto the cot. My sleep was cramped, like in a pressured corridor. When the bell rang, I would rise and report for work. I did my job thoroughly. The women guards didn't beat me or torment me. My contact with my fellow prisoners was little. They sat for hours after work and talked. Sometimes, at twilight, I would hear their confessions, sounding to me like yearnings that no longer touched upon life.

Once, at lunch, one of the prisoners asked me, "Katerina, how did you have the courage?"

"I don't know," I answered her.

That was the truth. My life was truncated, as though it no longer belonged to me, but I myself, wonder of wonders, stood on my own feet.

The women prisoners didn't abuse or mock me. One has to be wary of a woman capable of carving up a corpse into twenty-four pieces, I heard them whispering. Most of them were imprisoned, as I found out in the course of time, for poisoning or throwing acid. There were only two real murderesses, and I, it turned out, was one of them. The commandant summoned me and asked, "Do you have relatives?"

"I haven't. My parents died, and I was an only daughter."

"What are you laughing about?"

"The phrase 'only daughter' struck me as funny."

"Did you have other relatives?"

"My father had some bastards, but I didn't know them," I said, and kept on laughing.

"People don't laugh here. Get out of the room," they ordered me, and I left.

I rued my laughter, but I couldn't control myself. Before my eyes I saw my father's two redheaded bastards on the narrow wagon, the way I had seen them many years ago.

Although everyone here is sentenced to many years of imprisonment, still they count the days, the months, and the years. I was so hollow that the whole matter of time didn't concern me. I worked like a machine, and at the sound of the bell at night, I would put my tools down in the storeroom and report for roll call. After dinner they closed the sheds, and I would fall on my bunk like a sack.

The days passed, and one day was like the other. The women prisoners who worked outside used to talk of the summer sun and the harvests. Here, between the walls, it was very cold even when the sun shone. Everything absorbs the cold. But to me, to tell the truth, nothing was disturbing.

Once a month there were visits. Everyone looked forward to them, even putting on makeup. There was no one to visit me, and I was content that I didn't have to undergo that embarrassment. The visits left a layer of oppression and sadness. After the visits, the prison would be stirred up all night long.

"What are you thinking about?" One of the women prisoners surprised me while I was scouring the floor.

"I'm not thinking, I'm tired."

"It seemed to me that you were thinking."

"What is there to think about?" I said, trying to end the conversation.

The woman, my age, told me that she had already been imprisoned in that jail for six years and she had another seventeen years before her.

"What were you sent to jail for?" I asked, and I regretted it immediately.

"For throwing acid," she said, and smiled a strange smile.

Before getting married, she too had worked for Jews for many years. I immediately saw that she remembered her years with the Jews fondly, and like me, she had first worked for an observant family and then in the city for nonreligious Jews.

"They were my nicest years," she said, and tears welled in her eyes.

That is how the friendship between us began. Her name

was Sigi. In the winter, in the darkness and chill, we would bring up memories of Hanukkah and Purim; in the spring, of Passover and Shavuot. On Yom Kippur she would wrap herself in a shawl and fast. Had it not been for the boy who seduced her, had it not been for that cheat, she would have remained with the Jews forever.

Thus, miraculously, I found a secret tunnel to return to my loved ones. One evening I saw Henni. She knew what had happened to me and how I had landed there. I told her that there was no remorse in my heart. I was prepared for a long life in prison, without any illusions.

"Where do you get that faith?" Henni asked me.

"From my mother." I didn't hesitate.

"Strange," said Henni. "You didn't love your mother."

"I didn't know how to love her."

"And now you love her?"

"Now she's within me."

Barely had I pronounced those words when darkness covered that clear vision, and I sank down into the abyss.

21

WHILE THE WORK WORE THE days out, the cold made the nighttime hours infinitely long, and still I would wake each morning standing in line. There's no limit to how much a person can endure. I felt, sometimes, that changes were taking place in my body. My legs swelled up and the veins turned blue on my hands, but I had no pains. I worked from morning to night. At night I would stand on my feet and say to myself, Another day. The thoughts shriveled up in my head, like a hollowed pumpkin.

"Were you married?" Sigi asked me.

"No, but I had a child."

"Good for you."

Later she told me about her first days with the Jews, how she was afraid of them, and how she got over her fear. In the first winter she had come down with pneumonia, and she was sure they would fire her right away, but the Jews surprised her and took care of her. The first summer she met Herz Reiner, a young, nonreligious Jew, a student in Lemberg, who courted her with frightening gentleness.

"Wouldn't you like to go back to them?"

"I would."

Sigi was tall and strong and full of contradictions. "I love the Jews," she used to say. "But it's too bad they're Jews. If they weren't Jews, I would love them even more. They are special creatures. I love contact with them."

"Would you have married Herz Reiner?" My tongue egged me on.

"That's something else. A woman has to get married in the church. We sin and love young Jews, but the church doesn't love them. We have to marry people like ourselves."

"So you don't love them."

"I'm a Ruthenian, my dear, a Ruthenian wild beast. The Jews are another race. We can be amazed by them, sleep with them, love them, and curse them, but not marry them. We're different. What can you do? It's not our fault. That's how the Creator made us."

I liked Sigi. I didn't talk about everything with her, but I felt that we were attached to a memory full of warmth and sin, and that feeling gave us a kind of hidden advantage. We didn't talk about it to anyone, and not much between ourselves, but we enjoyed each other's company.

At night there was lots of talk. There were nights when they got carried away and talked about failed loves, and there were nights when they talked about harsh and vicious parents, or sometimes about brothers and sisters, and there were nights when they talked only about the Jews, and those were the liveliest nights of all. All of them had worked for Jews. And there were some whose fathers and forefathers had worked for the same family.

To steal from a Jew's house, that was a craft a person

learned over the years. It wasn't easy to steal from Jews, they were alert and quick, but if you confused them, it was quite possible. After a year or two, one knew all the secrets—when they prayed and when they mated. On the holidays they were all in the synagogue, and that was the time to rifle through the drawers. To steal from a Jew's house was a special kind of pleasure, almost like making love, declared one of them, and she made the women all laugh. Love affairs with Jews—that was also a matter they liked to explore. In that matter, there were some differences of opinion. Some women were sure that there was nothing like the Jews' love; they were clean and gentle and never would abuse a woman. Others held that their manners were too refined. A woman needs a beast of the field, not caresses and whispers.

Meanwhile, they informed me that my lawyer had come to visit. Visiting hours were tense. Within a short time you had to take everything in and tell everything, and all through a narrow barrier. The shouts were deafening. My lawyer got permission to see me in a guardroom, not with everyone else.

Since the trial his hair, or rather, the remnants of his hair, had gone gray. He was short and balding, but no change had occurred in his expression, soft and attentive. "I've wanted to come to see you for a long time, but I couldn't manage," he apologized. He had brought me a package of sweets and a jar of jam. Meanwhile, he told me that he had managed to recover the jewels that Henni had left me from the agency that had confiscated them. From now on they would be in the prison office, and when the time came and

I was freed, they would be returned to me, "And you'll have a penny to keep body and soul together."

"No need," I said, very stupidly.

"A person never knows what the days have in store for him."

Now he, too, seemed embarrassed. Perhaps he was disappointed because I hadn't appreciated his efforts enough. To correct the impression, I said, "Everything is fine with me." And that was the end of my words. He didn't know what to say either, and he got to his feet. No one urged us to finish the conversation, but I, for some reason, hurried back to the shed.

At night I continued digging down in search of a path to my dear ones. It seemed to me, for some reason, that if I could get to Henni, I could get to them all. That feeling led me astray. The nights grew completely opaque—not a slit and no light. Only darkness on top of darkness, and here, among the bunks, as in every tavern, they would curse and blame the Jews. If it weren't for the Jews, everything would be different. They must be exterminated, wiped off the face of the earth. There was no false note in those voices. They sounded as clearly as the mooing of a cow, and sometimes like a coarse folk song.

In my heart I knew that those voices didn't have the power to hurt my dear ones, but nevertheless I wasn't at ease. Who knows what harm a curse can do? My dear ones were wandering in the world of truth, laid bare, souls without bodies, and here the evil ones stood and reviled them day and night.

I hadn't feared in vain. The next day I learned that a pogrom had taken place in one of the villages near the prison. The killing wasn't very great, but there were many wounded. One of the jailers reported the details, and the news spread quickly. Apparently, the booty was plentiful this time. Now the peasants wouldn't need the Jews' stores anymore; they would have their own cloth, their own sugar, and high shoes of every type and size. Late that night a bottle of vodka passed from hand to hand. Everyone was happy that at long last they were letting the Jews have it.

At Passover, when it was permitted to give the women prisoners clothes and food, Jewish coats were already visible—lace dresses and woollen stockings and also a few new girdles. Everybody was happy, and they all tried them on.

"Why are you all alone?" One of the prisoners turned to me.

"I miss people." The words came out of my mouth.

"You should forget everything. Everything that was is as if it never were."

"And don't you remember?"

"Certainly I remember, but right away I say to myself, You mustn't remember. I've ordered my sisters and cousins not to come visit me. If I'm set free, I'll go visit them. They don't owe me anything. Visits just drive a person out of his mind. I would forbid visits. I don't miss anything anymore. I did what I had to do, and now I can sit at ease."

"What did you do?" I asked.

"I murdered my husband. Only you and I did the job all the way. The others just tried it and felt sorry about it." A spark lit her eyes.

The prison was well guarded, but news still slipped in through every crack. The day before, we had heard that

Sigi's husband had been killed in a tavern. Everyone was pleased and drank, and I too joined in the pleasure. Sigi got drunk and in her drunkenness she announced, "I love our Lord Jesus with a great, powerful love. He is our Lord, He is our Savior. I knew He would take vengeance for me. Now the time has come for the Jews who killed God. I've worked for the Jews a lot and I stole a lot of money from them, but I'll never forgive them for killing our Lord. How did those children of Satan dare to murder Him, for He is love and He is grace. God won't forgive them. He has prepared a great revenge for them. You'll see!"

She talked so much she vomited and turned as white as a sheet, but she didn't stop cursing everyone who had tormented her throughout her life: her father and mother, her husband and children, the Jews and their cheating. If she hadn't included the chief guard of the prison in her curses, the night would have ended happily and everyone could have slept in peace, but since she did include her, the jailers immediately pounced on her, beat her, and dragged her to the guardroom. The prisoners' pleas were of no avail. That night she was tried and sent to solitary confinement, and that was the end of the great celebration.

22

AFTER SIGI LEFT SOLITARY CONFINEMENT, she never
ceased praying and crossing herself, proclaiming that Jesus
was standing at her right hand, the God of vengeance had
appeared, and now the hour of the Jews had come as well.
A kind of flame blew on her bony cheeks. The Ruthenian
she spoke had also changed. She talked like the old women
in the village, mentioning Jesus every time she spoke, and
the Holy Mother and the angels, who would overcome all
evil and the children of Satan.

I'd lost a friend. I spoke to her very seldom, but she, for
some reason, sought my company, reproaching me and re-
minding me that without faith there is no life and without
Jesus we are lost in this world. Her voice was frightening.
"You have been influenced by the Jews too much. They've
cast their spells upon you and ruined the pure faith in you.
The children of Satan know a woman's soul and they pur-
chase it easily. You mustn't feel sorry for them. They've
blackened the Ruthenian soul."

I slipped away from her, willing to work in the frozen

fields so as not to be near her. One night I couldn't bear it any longer, and I said to her, "What do you want from me?" She was startled and said, "Nothing. I love you. I want to return you to the bosom of faith. The children of Satan have harmed you."

"Don't spread that nonsense," I said, and I was scared by my own voice.

The warning worked. People, it seems, fear murderers, and I too was afraid of my voice. In court they had exhibited the jackknife I had used to murder the murderer, and they asked me if that indeed was the same jackknife. It was a simple jackknife that I had taken with me when I left Henni's house. There had been no reason for that little theft.

Afterward, the days were short. The cold was great, and the work exhausting. My thoughts shriveled, and my legs moved along as though by themselves. I was cut off from my own life and buried in a kind of hard hollowness. I wasn't angry and I didn't want anything. If they punished us with overtime, I would work without a word. Everyone used to wait for visiting days with impatience. I didn't look forward to them. My lawyer would come once a month and bring, as was his habit, a few sweets and some jam.

"How are the Jews?" I asked, not in my own voice.

The lawyer was surprised by my question and said, "Why do you ask?"

"Rumors are flying about here that they slaughtered them in the villages."

"Does that worry you?"

"Jews, you should know, are very close to me."

"You'd better think about happier things," he whispered.

"They are dear to me." A voice came from my throat.

"I don't understand what you're driving at."

"I love their little houses."

"Don't talk out loud," he cut me off.

"I love to talk Yiddish. I miss it, like the breath of life."

The lawyer got to his feet and said, "That's irrelevant. We'll talk about it later."

"I'm not afraid."

"Nevertheless."

"I won't stop loving them." I managed to get out that sentence before the visit was terminated.

Later, I knew that it wasn't Katerina speaking. When Katerina is connected with her dear ones, her voice is full, her vocabulary different, and her feelings radiate from her body; but when she is cut off from them, she is like anyone else, weary and depressed.

That winter was very long. Occasionally, strong feelings would assail me, acute beliefs that would make my head spin till I felt faint. There were moments when I was very close to my dear ones, a great and very private closeness, especially to Benjamin, my little angel. That winter I told one of the women prisoners, "I don't need Jesus. I have my own Jesus." I didn't know what I was talking about, but they allowed me opinions and beliefs. People are cautious with murderers.

But most days I was depressed and kept to myself. My vision was diminished, my ears grew deaf, and I was sealed up like a wall. When they put out the lights, I curled up in my coat like an abandoned animal. The morning didn't inspire me with will or faith; I would dress and report for roll call as if it were an extension of a restless sleep. For a long time we would wait for the truck, and when it came at last, the women prisoners hurried to clamber aboard, knocking each other over in their rush. The truck was closed with a tarpaulin, and it was warmer there.

"Start working. That'll warm you up," said the old guard. He didn't beat us, but he berated us, saying that man was born to toil, there was no sin without punishment, and that one must accept punishment with love. The guards weren't evil spirits but human beings who did their duty. This world was only a corridor to the anteroom. Without doubt, there was a religious tinge to his words. Sometimes that tone evoked a thread of awe as in the priest's funeral prayers.

For six hours we would extract beets from the frozen earth. The spades were dull, but nevertheless our limbs did the impossible, bringing the beets up from their icy beds. After a few hours, there would be a pile of white beets. In the afternoon they brought us soup and a crust of bread. The food was tasteless, but a person can get used to anything. Sometimes a woman would despair of her life and flee, but not for long. The gendarmes would find her.

"Why not accept torments with love?" the old guard would preach his sermon to us all.

"These aren't torments, that's just humiliating," one of the women prisoners answered him blandly.

Nothing mattered to me. In those dark and opaque days, I did what I had to do. I didn't complain and I didn't make accusations. But occasionally, in the winter—and this happened several times—a kind of malicious joy would spread and grate upon my nerves. The pain was great, but I restrained myself. In the end I couldn't bear it anymore. I raised my voice and shouted, "Silence!"

"What do you want?" a prisoner asked impudently.

"Not to talk."

"Me?"

"You."

People treat murderers with respect. Not even the women guards yelled at me, but in my heart I knew my strength wasn't my own. Only when I was close to my dear ones did I have a voice, and there was awe in me.

At the end of the winter a lot of stolen shirts and sweaters reached us. Everyone was happy, but they didn't show it. "Don't put on that shirt. Katerina is roaming about." I would hear the whisper, my small revenge in this darkness.

23

IN APRIL THE DAYS WERE BRIGHT, the mornings very cold, but in the afternoons the sun would come down and warm us. We worked in open fields and we would return drunk with the pure air. Had it not been for a few escapes, the days would have passed uneventfully. After every escape came the beatings and the screaming. The chief guard, a sturdy, cruel woman, was responsible for the beatings; she beat with lust and devotion. She didn't torment murderesses, but she wheedled them, "Why face trials? Solitary confinement is no Garden of Eden, believe me."

Time vanished in the daily schedule. Your previous life grew ever more distant and vague, as though it wasn't your own. A prisoner came back to the shed after a day's work and sought nothing but her bunk. One woman remembered that she once had been held back a class in school, and her father, a senior official in the local council, wept from sheer embarrassment.

"My father," she confessed to me, "was apparently a little Jewish. At any rate, there was something Jewish about him. Only Jews are capable of crying about something like that."

"He didn't beat you?"

"No, he just wept."

"Do you have good memories of your father?"

"No. His weeping frightened me. He was a stranger to us all."

"What makes you suspect him?"

"I don't know. As a young man, he worked for Jews, and so did his mother, my grandmother—for many years she worked for Jews. Jewish manners clung to them."

"But you loved him."

"I didn't know how to love him. He liked to sit in the garden for hours and gaze around. I was afraid of him. In truth, we were all afraid of him. The Jews had a bad influence on him."

"Is he still living?"

"He died a year ago. I asked to attend the funeral, but they didn't let me. It's better they didn't. Everyone would have looked at me with pity. I don't like to be pitied. A person should suffer in silence."

Thus, from the thick depths, little trills rose up. Those whispers were absorbed very well in the shed, but they had the power to move one for a moment.

"How much more time do you have left?"

"I don't count. Anyway, I won't live to be freed."

I kept my secrets, and I didn't reveal them. Only with my lawyer would I exchange a few sentences and be moved. Once a month, he came to visit and brought me fruits that were in season. He was fifty, but his tattered clothing made him look older. If I could have done it, I would have laundered his shirt, pressed his suit, and polished his shoes. His loyalty pained me.

"How are the Jews in the villages?" I asked, not in my own voice.

"Why are you asking?"

"Because I'm afraid."

"A person should worry about himself. You have enough problems of your own."

Everything that happened in the villages was well known here—a robbery or murder every month. Jewish clothes came in regularly, even a pair of candlesticks. If I had money, I would have bought the clothes from the women and put them on my bunk. At night I would breathe in the starch hidden in their fabrics. I missed the village Jews—their little stores that gave off an odor of sunflower oil, the children racing about in the courtyard, the silence of Sabbaths and holidays, the old Jews standing at street corners and looking about in wonderment. For a long while they would stand, and suddenly a smile would rise to their lips, then they picked up their feet and disappeared. For hours I would observe their birdlike way of walking. I always had the feeling that they were linked to blue and silent worlds.

But, even to myself, I didn't reveal the great secret. My Benjamin had gone up to heaven and he was the true Jesus. Jesus in the churches has rosy cheeks, plump arms, and his whole look is annoyingly self-righteous. A kind of revolting spirituality. A fake angel. But my Jesus had been in my womb, and to this day he fills me. My Benjamin doesn't look self-righteous like the icons in the church. My Benjamin used to bite. They were sharp but sweet bites, sealed into my flesh to this day. My Benjamin would stick out his tongue and tease me, and sometimes he hid under the table and called in a chirping voice, "Mommy's a mouse. Mommy has a tail." Benjamin was mischievous. Without his mischief, I wouldn't have known how much light there was in him. Sometimes I said to myself, Where is my mischievous one? There were days when I saw him in the midst of a field or among the open containers, the ladles, and the coarse words. He was present everywhere. I don't like it when people bow and scrape. After kneeling and bowing down, a person is capable of dreadful actions. On Sunday, after prayers, they used to behead animals for the big meals.

"Why are you so quiet, Katerina? What are you thinking about?" The chief guard spoke to me in a motherly tone.

"I'm not thinking."

"But something seems to be disturbing you. You can tell me. We no longer punish people for thoughts."

"I have no complaints."

They were afraid of me. One of the prisoners refused to sleep next to me, and when they forced her, she wept like a child who had been spanked. The chief guard's scoldings were no use. In the end, she sat next to her and spoke softly: "You have nothing to fear. Katerina won't do you any harm. Murderers only murder once, and after that they're quiet and pleasant. I have lots of experience. Quite a few murderesses have been jailed here." Strangely, those words calmed her, and she brought in her belongings and made the bed beside me.

"What's your name?" I asked her.

At the sound of my question her shoulders tensed, and she stepped back, saying, "Sophia."

"Why are you scared?"

"I'm not afraid, I'm just shivering."

You have nothing to fear, I wanted to tell her, but I knew my words would make her tremble even more.

"It's hard for me to stop shivering. My body shivers by itself."

"We mustn't be afraid of each other," I said for some reason.

"I'm not afraid anymore, but it's hard for me to stop shivering. What can I do?"

Her face was disheveled and wrinkled. You could see that she had been afraid all her life. First, she had been scared of her mother and father, later, of her husband. In her great fear, she had tried to murder her husband. Now she was in jail and afraid of her cellmates. The chief guard didn't spare her. She beat her, but not hard. She tortured her, not for her sins but for her fears. "You mustn't be afraid of people, you understand?"

"I'm not afraid anymore," she assured me.

"Don't tell me you're not afraid. You're all fear."

"I don't know what to do," she finally admitted.

"You have to say to yourself, There is God in heaven and He is the king of kings. He knows every secret and only Him do I fear. All the rest is illusion. Do you understand me?"

Sophia's behavior was exceptional. The women prisoners usually accepted blows in silence, sat in solitary confinement without screaming, but there were days when the chief guard went out of her mind, casting dread on everyone, and then screams rose up to heaven.

24

YEARS PASSED, and a woman with the same name as mine arrived here. She was younger than I, from my village, and glad to see me. She told me at length about a quarrel over property, about the living, and about the dead. My murder had apparently made a big impression in the village. As after every horrible act, the village split into two camps. Some people thought I was justified and they blamed the Jews for whom I had worked, while others blamed me and my wanton character. She herself had been sentenced to life in prison for injuring her husband. Her husband had jabbed her with a pitchfork in the barn. She had snatched the tool from his hands and, with the very same tool, struck and wounded him.

I remembered her but not clearly. Our houses in the village were far apart, but sometimes we would meet in the pasture, at weddings, or in church. Even then she carried the anxious look of a hunted animal. I had not seen my village for years and it had even been erased from my dreams,

but suddenly it rose again to life, a painful rebirth, with all
its odors and colors.

"You haven't changed," she told me.

"How is that?"

"I would have known you right away."

I remembered her. She had been about five, dressed in a
long linen gown and standing next to the large animals and
staring at them with a look of amazement. Something of
that look remained in her eyes.

"What do people do here?" she asked me in a homey
voice, the way you ask people in the village.

"They work." I tried to make the moment milder.

She cried, and I didn't know what to say to her. In the
end I told her, "Don't cry, dear. Lots of people have entered
and left this place. A life sentence isn't the final word. There
are early releases and pardons."

"Everybody hates me, even my children."

"You have nothing to worry about. God knows the whole
truth. Only He can judge you." Barely had I pronounced
the name of God when the anguish was wiped from her
face, her eyes opened wide, and she looked at me with that
gaze from her childhood.

"I thought about you a lot," she said.

"There's nothing to worry about, we're not all alone."

"Who could have imagined we'd meet here?"

"It's not such a dreadful place," I went on, to distract
her.

"Does anyone visit here?" the poor thing kept on asking.

"There's no need for visits. Here a person minds his own
business."

"A Jewish lawyer defended me. I don't believe in the Jews.

They always talk a lot, but their mouths and hearts are not the same. A life sentence is better than being defended by Jews. They run around everywhere."

I let her hatred seethe and sensed that the seething eased her pain. Afterward, I offered her an illicit sip of liquor. The drink calmed her, and her face returned to her. She said, "Thanks, Katerina. May God watch over you. Without you, what would I do here?"

"What did they say about me in the village?" I tried to amuse her.

"That the Jews put a spell on you."

"Do you believe that?"

We both laughed.

The days passed, and no one came to visit her. In the winter there were hardly any visits. The prison is remote and access difficult. Only my lawyer showed up, appearing as regularly as clockwork.

"Why take the trouble?" I reprimanded him.

"I'm your lawyer, aren't I? Doesn't a lawyer have to find out how his clients are?"

"True, but you have to watch your health. Health comes before everything."

During the past two years he had aged. His clothing had become ragged, his lower lip, which had been a bit swollen and blue, seemed to have become bluer still. A cigarette was always stuck to it. On that cold day his face expressed neither goodheartedness nor wisdom; a kind of iciness suffused it. The whole time, he rubbed his hands together and said, "It's cold, cold out." Why did you come then? I wanted to scold him, but instead I said, "In your office, there's a heater."

"What office are you talking about? It's been a long time since I've had an office."

"You need an office, don't you?" I said, and I didn't know what I was talking about.

"I have no need for an office anymore," he said, waving his right hand.

The winds blew in, hurling their drafts into the exposed anteroom. I remembered my first meeting with him in the midst of the angry crowd of gendarmes, wardens, and attorneys. He had seemed shorter than all of them to me, thin and embarrassed.

"I'm your lawyer," he'd introduced himself. "I'll try to defend you with all my might. Your case is a complicated one, but we'll prevail."

"What can I give you?" I had asked him then, very stupidly.

"There's no need for anything."

Now the same man was standing before me, only more impoverished. The cigarette on his blue lip seemed to be stuck there from the time I'd first seen him.

"Where do you live?"

"I have a room in town. My parents live in a village. I sometimes visit them. They aren't pleased with me."

"Why aren't they pleased with you?"

"Once they wanted me to marry," he said, and smiled.

"You didn't miss anything."

"My parents had great hopes for me. I'm an only son. They worked hard all their lives, and they invested their savings in me so that I could study at the university. I wanted to study painting, but they didn't consent. They didn't appreciate painting, so I studied what they wanted."

"You're a successful lawyer." I tried to encourage him.

"It's hard to say I'm successful. I don't have an office, and I don't know how to collect fees, either. But I'm not going to change, apparently."

A kind of spirit seized me, and I told him, "You defended me excellently. With all your might."

"In my opinion, you should have been found innocent."

"I'm not sure."

"I am."

He fastened his coat and was about to leave. Buttoned up now, he looked even shorter. I very much wanted to give him something of my own for the road, but I didn't have anything. "Don't go out in the storm." I wanted to delay him.

"I'm not afraid. An hour's walk—and I'm at the railroad station."

"It's not worth taking the risk in this weather." I spoke to him in an old-fashioned way. The guard in the hut didn't press us. In that season, everyone is busy keeping his limbs warm. The watchman was also stamping his feet.

"Don't go to the village. You won't change your parents, and they won't change you. Everyone to his own fate."

He was surprised by my voice for a moment and said, "All these years I caused them only unhappiness. I very much want to visit them, but I don't dare. It's hard for me to bear their looks. They don't reprimand me anymore. My father even gave me a little money—but it isn't right to take money from an old man. They've worked hard all their days."

"Are you observant?"

"You've touched a sore point. It's hard for my parents to accept that their only son is making his way through the world without faith. If I were successful at my profession, they would certainly forgive me."

At that moment I felt a strong physical attraction for that little, troubled man, the way I had felt once toward Sammy. My dear, I was about to tell him, I'm willing to be your servant, your concubine, to clean your room and wash your shirt. My body's not holy. I love you because you have a light that warms my soul. It's hard for me to bear the coarseness of the women here.

"I'll be seeing you," he said, and raised his hand.

"When?"

"I'll come in a month."

"Thank you. I'll be expecting you."

"To my regret, I didn't bring you good news."

"But your very coming, your being here . . ."

At that moment a great storm was raging outside, a black storm. Through the cracks in the door I could see him as he headed off, and the wind swung him on its wings.

25

THE DAYS ADVANCED HEAVILY, as though they were tethered to a sluggish locomotive. The winter was long and its darkness was great, and the summer was hardly felt. One day was like the other; there was no end to the days. Nevertheless, year pursued year. A person no longer sought closeness to anyone. Almost nobody talked to me. A murderess is a murderess, I heard more than once. I didn't answer, and I didn't insult. I was attached to my secret by an umbilical cord, and from there I drew patience. I had a family hidden from all eyes. Now my lawyer had joined it. For months, he didn't come to visit me.

Sometimes I saw him in the image of John the Baptist, standing by the waters of the Prut and pouring water on people's heads. That task doesn't suit you, I remarked to him. And what task does suit me? he asked without turning his head. You're the court-appointed lawyer for the poor and the downcast; they are certainly waiting for you. You're right, my dear, you're absolutely right. But you mustn't forget that a year ago I was dismissed from my job. But if my new task doesn't please you, I shall return to my old one. I hope they won't kill me. If you're afraid, don't go there, I was about to tell him, but I didn't have the chance. He disappeared from before my eyes. I didn't understand the meaning of that dream. I missed him and his cringing movements, and every month I expected him.

Outside, they had begun looting Jewish shops once again, and no small amount of the booty continued to arrive. One of Sigi's aunts brought her a poplin blouse. I saw immediately that it was a Jewish blouse. Sigi wore it, and her mood improved. It was very hard for me to bear the way she looked in that blouse, but I restrained myself and didn't say a thing. But one evening I couldn't control myself and I said to her, "That blouse doesn't suit you."

"Why?"

"Because it belongs to the Jews."

"So what?"

"You mustn't wear the clothing of tortured people."

"Jews don't scare me."

My hands shook. I was alarmed by the tremor, because I felt that it was a violent one, that I didn't have the power to subdue it. Sigi apparently felt that she'd gone too far and said, "Why get angry for nothing?" Later, she said, as though by the way, "I see you still love Jews."

"I don't understand." I feigned innocence.

"I have a strong aversion to the Jews. The Jews, to tell the truth, never cheated me or bothered me, but I still feel no pity for them. Once, I even had a Jewish lover, unquestionably a sweet young man. We used to go out on walks, to the movies, and cafés. I knew I'd never again know love like that, but I still wasn't at ease. The Jews make my heart restless. I feel guilty. Maybe you can explain that to me. The Jews drive me out of my mind."

I looked at her and I saw she was telling the truth. Anyway, there was no malice, just a desire to solve a difficult riddle. "Strange," she said. "At night I'm not angry either at myself or at my mother, not even at my husband, who abused me. I get angry at the Jews. They drive me out of my mind. Do you understand?"

"But they didn't hit you."

"Correct, you're absolutely right. But what can I do? It's a fact: Everybody hates them."

To be at peace with myself, I told Sigi, "Don't speak ill of the Jews. That kind of talk drives me mad. It's hard for me to control myself."

"Would you hit me?" She was alarmed.

"Not I," I said as though to myself, "but my hands."

"Ignore me."

"The poplin blouse you're wearing makes me crazy."

"For your sake, I won't wear it."

"Thank you very much."

The days raked us into their flow like beasts. We worked. With our last strength we dislodged beets from the frozen soil. The head jailer used to beat the weak women mercilessly. The screams would shatter our ears, but our hearts knew no pity. From month to month my heart grew harder. My life was nothing but movements, and at night I would sink down on my cot like all the rest and fall asleep. Fatigue was so powerful that it conquered me completely. My contact with other worlds was limited and rare. Only occasionally would I clench my fists and sense my strength, but very quickly they relaxed.

In my heart I secretly envied all the women who sat and chatted at night, quarreling and cursing. I had no words, as though they had withered within me. Even the simple numbers scrawled on the wall made me dizzy. Were it not for the work, were it not for that curse, I would have been buried in sleep.

One evening, after the lineup, Sigi approached me and said, "Katerina, permit me to say a word to you. Don't get angry at me and don't hit me."

"Don't say it to me." I turned down her request.

"I can't keep it in. It's weighing on my heart like a stone."

"But why do you have to irritate me?" I said, and my hands clenched.

"I have to."

"You don't have to. You can control your mouth."

Hearing my words, she lowered her head and burst into tears. "Do what you want. Hit me as much as you want to. Your attitude toward the Jews frightens me more than the prison, more than the jailer, more than solitary confinement."

"Shut up!" I cried to her.

But she didn't keep quiet, and it was clear to me that she was prepared to die beneath my fists. Yet she would not conceal her truth from me. Her weeping rose, and as it rose, my hands weakened.

26

I READ THE PSALMS and prayed to God not to lead me into temptation. Aside from the Old and New testaments, books were forbidden. Only there, in that darkness, did I learn to pray. I am not sure whether it was conventional prayer, but I felt devotion to the words and that devotion sometimes drew me out of the darkness in which I was lying.

But the sights one sees are stronger than the soul's yearnings. The women's wing was flooded with blouses, sweaters, pillows, and candlesticks. That loot blinded me. Everyone received gifts, even the women who hadn't received anything at first. Lipsticks, bottles of cologne, and a few packets of soap also made their way in here.

The chief jailer averted her eyes from several infractions, and it was clear that a new regime had arisen. The face of things outside had changed. All the women were awaiting a tall, strong man who would come and break down the iron doors and free them. A kind of dark joy enveloped the women by their bedsides. They laughed wantonly and flounced about in the Jewish clothes.

Sophia, who slept in the neighboring bed, got a long silk dress from her sister, a necklace, and two jackets. Her lust for new clothing calmed her fears. Now she strutted about with her neck outstretched like a peacock's. "Don't wear those clothes," I asked her, but she ignored my request.

The long dress imbued her with courage. She spoke like a peasant woman about to marry her daughter off in the city, as though her fears were forgotten. My hands shook, but I restrained myself. Finally, I couldn't contain myself and I said, "At thy enemies' fall shalt thou not rejoice."

"So it's forbidden to dress up?" she said impudently.

"It's permitted to dress up, but it's forbidden to rejoice."

"I hate sanctimonious people."

"I'm a simple woman, not sanctimonious. I've never been sanctimonious in my life. I didn't preserve my body for myself, but I won't wear the clothes of persecuted people. It's forbidden to wear the victims' clothes. Torments are holy."

"Why do you always defend the Jews?"

"I was talking about taking malicious pleasure."

"I can't live on proverbs. With me, feeling comes before everything."

My arms were already charged with power, but I, for some reason, still checked myself. But she went on, saying, "We're talking openly. Let's not hide our hatred." I couldn't bear it any longer. I lifted my arms and knocked her down. No one came to her assistance, and I knew no one would. I stood there and beat her resoundingly with my fists. She was bleeding when the chief jailer rescued her.

They don't put true murderesses in solitary confinement but in a special room with a bunk and sink. Before long the chief jailer motioned to pack up my things and move them to the special room. I did so, saying nothing.

"Why did you beat her?" the chief jailer asked me without raising her voice.

"She drove me crazy."

"You have to restrain yourself." She spoke like a woman who knew people's weaknesses.

"I wanted to hit her for a long time."

"Now you'll have to live in total isolation."

"I'm already used to not talking."

"A person still needs a little company, isn't that so?"

"I can be by myself."

"I'll come and visit you," said the chief jailer, and locked the door.

A new life opened before me. Indeed the room was very narrow, but when I stood on my bed I could fill my gaze with fields and meadows. Moreover, the room wasn't entirely isolated. In the evening I caught the prisoners' voices, and from their voices I learned that the Jews had already been driven out of their homes and the looting was continuing. People celebrated with malicious joy until late at night.

Only after midnight was I with myself and my dear ones. The gates of the land opened before me, and Benjamin came toward me, crawling under the table. I saw the shadows of his hands, and the room filled with his laughter. He had not grown since he was taken from me. Now his look is like that of a little Jesus, clasped in his mother's arms, just like the wooden relief carved by an artist in the chapel. I bent my knee and called to him, "Benjamin, my dear." But I was immediately alarmed by the words *my dear*, because I never called him my dear. "Benjamin," I say. "Your mother is talking. Why are you hiding?" I stepped back a little, waiting for him to appear, but he didn't come out from under the table. I gathered my strength and took a few steps on my knees, saying, "Benjamin, I'm your mother. Don't you remember my voice?"

"I'm here." I heard his voice, familiar to the marrow of my bones.

"I want to see you."

"I'm right at your side." I heard his laugh.

I tried to lift my knees, but my knees wouldn't come away from the floor.

When I woke up the next day, I felt his body in my arms.

That morning they placed us, Sophia and me, in the same row. There were still some black-and-blue marks on her face from the blows I had showered upon her. She begged and pleaded not to be put next to me. A few of the prisoners felt sorry for her and were willing to trade places, but the jailer stubbornly refused. Finally, she had no choice but to take the spade in her hand and force it into the hard earth. She worked at my side in dread, without lifting her head and without uttering a sound.

"Why aren't you talking?" I addressed her.

She was alarmed. She raised her head and said, "I'm afraid. They put you in solitary confinement because of me."

"I won't hit you again."

"But I'm afraid."

"For my part, I won't hit you. I swear by my departed parents that I won't hit you. Solitary confinement isn't so bad. And how are things in the sheds?" I tried to continue the conversation.

"Everything's fine. The mood is good. The Germans are

doing great things on the front, driving the Jews out of the villages. There's lots of booty. Everybody's getting something out of it." For a moment she was swept away by that enthusiasm, but she immediately noticed her error, took her head in both hands, and shouted, "I made a mistake again! I sinned again!"

"What's the matter?" I tried to calm her down.

"I always annoy you."

"Today you're not annoying me anymore. You can talk as much as you please."

"I won't talk. I'm afraid to talk."

"I'm a Ruthenian daughter of Ruthenians, and nothing Ruthenian is alien to me. When I die, they'll lay me next to my mother and father. You mustn't be afraid."

"I'm afraid. What can I do? It's hard to stop fear." She was relieved, apparently, and she wept. For a moment I was about to put my hands on her shoulders, but in my heart I knew that would frighten her very much. She wept for a long time and finally immersed herself in her work, not speaking to me again until the evening.

27

DURING THE DREADFUL NINETEEN FORTIES I almost didn't write, and what I did write, I destroyed with my own hand. I worked without fatigue, as if the beet field were my own farm. The trains, which would pass before us, were crammed with Jews. All the women were happy that we would be rid of them once and for all.

They would fight among themselves over every piece of cake, blouse, or ointment. The cells in solitary confinement were full, and shouts were heard day and night. The jailers used to spray water into the cells to silence the women. During the nineteen forties, darkness descended upon me. All my bonds with my dear ones were severed. I knocked on the doors at night in vain. No sign, or any word, came from them, only darkness upon darkness and a great abyss.

At that time a skin disease spread over my body. The disease ravaged my face and made it hideous. "The monster," the prisoners used to whisper. My face was covered with red and pink spots, and my hands swelled. I was like an uninhabited cave, with no sights and no thoughts. True, they still didn't dare offend me and they didn't abuse me. Mainly, I worked alone, and if they attached a prisoner to me, she refrained from talking to me. Sometimes the chief jailer would come into my room and exchange a few words. Once she asked me if I wanted to return to the shed. "I'm better off here," I said, and she didn't bother me about that anymore.

Sweet and sourish smells wafted in from every side. I didn't know that was the smell of death. Everybody else knew, and they said it, that it was the smell of the Jews' death, but I refused to listen. I was certain they were wicked hallucinations.

In the early morning, while I was still pulling beets out of the earth, long freight trains would pass by. The prisoners used to greet the trains with shouts of joy, "Death to the merchants, death to the Jews." They knew everything. Their senses were lively. They sat in prison, but they knew everything that was going on around them—how many Jews had been sent and how many were going to be sent. Each train aroused a wave of joy, and at night they would sing:

"Finally they're burning
Our Lord's killers and opposers,
The smell of those fires
is sweet perfume to our noses."

That was a mighty song that reverberated until late. The jailers ignored standing orders and let them sing. They sang enthusiastically, the way they sang Christmas carols, and they tapped their feet and bellowed.

And I, almighty God, I took care of myself. I was certain that pink, virulent sickness would do away with me. That concern filled my whole being. Now, when I think about my blindness and selfishness, shame devours me. Let me quickly add that it was then that I once again found a path to the Psalms. I clung to the holy words, and I used to pray for long hours. The verses would calm my fears. Forgive me, God, for that selfish prayer as well.

Day after day the trains rolled by. There was no longer any doubt that death was not far away. In the courtyard, wagons heaped with clothes stood abandoned. No one wanted them. Moisture ruined them, and within a matter of days they lost their shape. On visiting days, people no longer brought clothes but gold jewels.

At lunch, Sigi approached me and said, "It's hard for me to bear your silence, Katerina. Not many years ago we were friends. Why are you pushing me away? I have no one in this world."

"I'm not angry at you."

"Why won't you come back to us in the shed? It's easier together than alone. Isolation makes you sick."

"I need to be by myself. To sit quietly and heal my wounds."

"Come to us. We need you very much."

"Thanks, Sigi."

"We women are all responsible for each other, aren't we?"

"True." I said what I had to.

Sigi had grown old in the past two years. Her full face, which had known both lust and faith, had sagged. When the day came and she was set free, she wouldn't know what to do with her freedom. Her face had put on a prison mask, the same pallor and the same neglect. Now she still sang at night, but on the outside she wouldn't know how to open

her mouth. No wonder all her relatives had abandoned her
and her children had not even visited once.

"You're thinking about the Jews." She surprised me.

"True. How do you know?"

"You mustn't think about them. That's their fate. That's
God's will."

"I understand."

"We mustn't ask about what's above us and what's below
us. Do you understand?"

28

AGAIN, THE DAYS WERE BRIGHT and hot and I worked harvesting corn. The skin disease continued to spread over my face in a thick rash, and everyone avoided me. The chief jailer assigned me a corner of the field so I wouldn't have contact with anyone. After a day's work, I would return alone, and behind me, at a good distance, followed the jailer. If I hadn't been a murderess, they certainly would have freed me. They free afflicted people, but they are strict with murderesses.

Only the other Katerina, from my village, dared to approach me. I told her that it didn't hurt much and that I could bear it. It was a discomfort you could overcome. I was glad to have found the correct words. Katerina lowered her head, as though I had recited a verse from Scripture.

Poor Sophia, the woman I had beaten, called from a distance, "Katerina, for my part I forgive you for everything. If only we could see you healthy among us." She wore a broad peasant kerchief on her head, and she looked like a miserable servant.

The nights were hot and close, with no air to breathe. Like black snakes, the trains twisted through the valley. Prisoners no longer stood by the bars and shouted, "Death to the merchants, death to the Jews." Now there was no doubt that after the Jews were all dead, they would free all of us. We had to await their death patiently. Not many were left, and those few were being transported in trains. Through cracks in the wall I caught the whispers. It wasn't malice but tense expectation.

How correctly they had guessed only became known to me later. Even during that accursed summer I was cut off from all my dear ones. My isolation and illness surrounded me like a tight band. The fire was trapped in my bones, wiping out every part of me. My soul dried out from day to day in my swollen body.

And at night, strong flames would penetrate my sleep and lick my flesh. I was very close to death, but each time an escape opened before me. After all, prison isn't a sealed freight car. More than once during that long summer I wanted to loose the shackles from my hands, to grasp one of the prisoners and shake her powerfully. They used to grovel before the jailers like slaves, all for a bit of drink or some powder or cologne. One mustn't grovel, and one mustn't wish for other people's death. Death isn't the end. There are heights upon heights, cried all my limbs. My mother used to come back to my body and fill me with courage. My arms were ready for the struggle, but there was no strength in them. The prisoners knew that, and they didn't fear me anymore.

There was one very old woman in the sheds, a woman of about ninety, who had completed her prison term years earlier but refused to be set free and asked to stay. Her wish was granted, and she remained not only with the women of her generation but also those of the two following generations. She was the prison's memory. She recalled all the practices of earlier years—who was freed and when, who was sick and who was healed, who had a bitter fate and who was fortunate. But, mainly, she taught the prisoners patience. Patience is a holy virtue. When a person acquires that virtue, no harm can come.

Years earlier, her glance had encountered me, and she hated me. She immediately declared that my expression— though it was indeed a Ruthenian one, and you could see I had grown up in a good Christian home—something had become muddied there, irreparably. Poor Katerina tried to defend me, but the old woman stuck to her opinion: "The Jews have destroyed her soul, and she can never be redeemed." Since I had fallen sick, I became an example that she constantly cited. "You can see with your own eyes what the Jews did to her. Hell is roasting her in this world."

"How many trains went by last night?"

"Seven."

"I see they've picked up the pace." I heard Sigi's voice.

They all compared and counted. The trains passed through the valley with crisp speed, like red-hot bullets. I was shut off and heavy. If there was anyone I hated, it was that old woman. She didn't speak anymore but prophesied, and her prophecies were poisoned arrows. "In a little while," she used to whisper, "in a little while the end will come to all the killers of our Lord Jesus. One mustn't rush the end. Let things take their course. Everything is for the best."

Nobody realized how close the end was. One morning

we saw that there was no one on the towers. Black crows hopped on the flat roofs. The jailers had fled, too. Even the commissary had abandoned his storeroom. None of us could believe our eyes.

"There are no more Jews," announced the old woman. "Arise, women, and return to your homes." But no one dared get up. The sun was full and low, and a silence, like after a great war, was spread on the valley and on the barren ridges. Sigi stretched her hand, a large hand, through the bars of the window and said, "Everything has stopped moving."

29

I DIDN'T KNOW WHAT TO DO, and I walked out. I was at peace. Green meadows stood before me. The years in prison made my heart forget many people, but not the meadows. A few abandoned animals grazed in ditches. By the look of the animals, I knew that the year had been rainy, the crops had come along nicely and in season, and the harvest had been on time too. At harvest, my mother had been like a gale wind. She preferred hired workers to my father. My father knew nothing of devotion in his work. The older he grew, the lazier he became. My mother, in contrast, never rested. She used to work from morning to late at night. At the end of the harvest we would bring the sacks of grain to the flour mill, where the people squabbled and insulted each other. Once, I remember, a man was stabbed in the chest.

I turned and saw that the prison still stood in its place. From there it looked wretched. Seen together, the buildings seemed like the shelters peasants put up at harvest time. My fears had been unnecessary. The entire fortress looked precarious, and even the fences were very carelessly made.

I wanted, for some reason, to see what was left to me after all those confined years, and I could only see heaps of beets in the frost. All the people who had surrounded me, and there were years when I hadn't been isolated, had not even left the look of their faces in me, nor their smell.

Not far away, the women prisoners wandered off together, raising columns of dust with their steps. For a moment it seemed to me that everything would remain this way forever. I would look at them from a distance, and they would whisper to each other, and even if we moved apart, the distance between us would not be shortened. That thought made me tremble with an old kind of fear.

I walked toward the ditches. The cows lifted their heads, and I drew close and touched their skin. For years I hadn't touched an animal, not, in fact, since I had left the village. I fell to my knees and plucked handfuls of grass.

Contact with the fresh grass moved me, and I turned toward the hilltops. The hilltops reminded me of my aunt Fanka's house. Aunt Fanka, my mother's sister, was a very special woman. She lived outside the village, on a bare hilltop, and she didn't need people. I saw her just once, but her thin face remained stamped upon me. It had the kind of spirituality you don't find among Ruthenians. For years, her face hadn't reappeared to me, and suddenly, as though from the thickness of the dark, it rose up again.

At the foot of the hill stood a pond full to the brim. Ponds like that are found at the edges of every village. Here they water the animals, and here boys come to bathe. Once Waska had also drawn me to the pond. He was bashful and didn't stroke my breasts.

A few haystacks stood abandoned next to an oak. I ap-

proached them and said, "I'll rest awhile." The dry straw
made me sink into a deep doze, a slumber without visions.
At first it skimmed and floated, but it became heavy during
the night, pulling me downward. Had it not been for a
thirst that roused me from time to time, I doubt whether
I would have awakened.

Sudden rain forced me from the haystack, and I stood
under a tree. No one was within sight, just fields of yellowish
stubble with glowing hues like darkened amber. For many
years I had not seen a yellow like that. The fear of God fell
upon me, and I knelt.

The rain turned out to be a passing summer shower. The
clouds scattered, and the sun stood high in the heavens
again, a large, round sun of the kind that had shone upon
me in the meadows when I was a girl. Here too it grew
steadily lower, as though it were about to fall at my feet.
Suddenly, I knew that everything I saw was merely a frag-
ment of a vision whose beginning was far from me, whose
middle was within me, and what was revealed before me
now was merely an illuminated passage leading to a broad
tunnel. The light was strong and spilled out at my feet. It
seemed that I had stood in this place years ago but that life
had bustled about then, faces had surrounded me, and I had
examined them.

Toward evening a wagon drew up beside me. A peasant
woman, wrapped in a rustic blue kerchief, drove her horses
indolently. When she was close by, I asked, "Where is the
city?" I was immediately thunderstruck by the word I had
uttered.

"There's no city around here. You're in the heart of the

country, mother." She spoke to me in the old-fashioned
way, just the way we used to talk at home, in the heart of
the country.

"And where are the Jews?" I asked, and immediately knew
the question was out of place.

"Why do you ask, mother?" she answered me, and her
face, a young woman's face, appeared to me from inside the
kerchief.

"I don't know," I said.

After a moment of surprise, she said, "They took them
away."

"Where did they take them?" I asked again, not in my
own voice.

"To their fate, they took them, mother. To their fate.
Don't you know?" There was ingenuousness in her face.

"Aren't you afraid?" The words left my mouth.

"There's nothing to be afraid of, mother. God took them.
And where are you from, mother?"

"From the prison." I didn't hesitate.

"Thank God," she said, and crossed herself. "Praised be
God who frees the prisoners. Were you in for a long time?"

"More than forty years."

"God preserve us! Take a few of this season's fruits," she
said, offering me a handful of plums.

"Thank you, my child."

From the time I entered prison, I hadn't seen plums.
Sometimes a few withered apples would make their way
into the shed, and they would be gobbled down swiftly,
core and all. The sight of the plums moved me, as though
it were a gift from heaven.

"Thanks, my child, for this lovely gift. I shall never forget it. May the good Lord reward you for the kindness with all the good and lovely things He possesses."

"Thank you for the blessing," she said, and bowed as they do in the country.

"What's your name, mother?"

"Katerina."

"God almighty!" she said, opening her eyes wide. "You're Katerina the murderess!" Without a moment's delay, like someone who has met the devil himself on his way, she raised the whip and lashed the backs of the horses. The horses, startled by that sudden whipping, reared up on their hind legs and drew the wagon away with a rush.

30

I DIDN'T MOVE FROM WHERE I WAS. The lights of day mingled with the lights of night, and night in that season is as short as a heartbeat. You lay your head on the straw, and dawn already breaks out. I knew I had to do something, to move forward or to raise my voice, but the silence that surrounded me on all sides was great and thick and my legs were heavy, as though metal had been cast around them.

Some distance away wagons full of clover lumbered along. I saw that just an hour ago it had been mown, and soon the peasants would pile it in the broad feeding troughs. Children skipped in front of the wagon wheels the way I had done when I was their age. "Who's there?" I called out. Since my encounter with that peasant woman, I was attentive to every noise. In the villages they forgive murderers but not murderesses. Murderesses have been regarded as a horror and a curse from time immemorial. They are pursued to the death. A murderer, after he's served his sentence, returns to his village, marries, and fathers children, and no one reminds him of his deed. But a murderess is forever a murderess. I knew that and wasn't frightened. On the contrary, I had a strong desire to approach the wagons and feel the clover with my hands, but the wagons quickly passed me by.

Meanwhile, I remembered that during the long summer evenings the Jews used to come to the village and spread out their wares on hangers and improvised stands. And there were stands for special fruits, dates and figs, stands for creams and perfumes, household goods and furs from the city. In the summer twilight, the peddlers looked like ancient priests breathing enchantment into their belongings. That was the summer market, and everybody called it the Jews' long market. They sold all night, and toward morning the prices would drop to half. I didn't sleep during those nights, and my mother, who knew what I wanted, would drive me into the house with a stick. Nevertheless, I stole, sometimes together with Maria, but mostly alone. Everybody was drunk with the lights of the night at the summer market, and from the sparkling of the lake, which spread an enthralling glow. You could buy everything at that market— pumps and high-heeled shoes, beads, cloth, and even transparent silk stockings. My young head was not given over to wonders at that time. The urge to steal was stronger than everything, and I stole whatever came to hand. Poor Maria—at our last meeting at the station she wore a necklace around her neck, one we had stolen together from the Jews. She too is in the world of truth, and only the summer light, the eternal summer light, flows as it always used to flow.

I uprooted my legs and advanced. The night light grew stronger above me. I was thirsty. The years of hunger in prison hadn't left me with hunger, only thirst. I drank from the pond, and for the first time I saw my face: not Katerina of the meadows and not Katerina of the railroad station and not Katerina of the Jews. Very little hair remained on my head, and my face was thin and old.

Some distance away, on the hilltops, serene smoke rose in columns over the houses. I knew that everyone was seated at the table, and the lady of the house was serving fatback, cabbage, and potatoes. In the long summer evenings it's hard to sleep. Even babies in the cradle are awake and absorb the rustling of the night light. For an instant I forgot the many years, and I wrapped myself up in moments of peace that remained from my childhood.

But not for long. The smell of burning came to my nostrils. First it seemed that the smell was rising up from the ditches where the cows were grazing in the daylight. It wasn't a harsh or oppressive smell. For some reason it reminded me of the picnics that Maria and her companions used to have in the woody glens on summer days. The boys used to steal chickens from the village, slaughter them, and roast the meat on coals. I was about twelve years old, and the sight of the slaughtered fowl on the coals frightened me greatly. Maria, from sheer anger, used to threaten me, saying, "You mustn't be scared. If slaughtered chickens scare you, who'll save you from the murderers?" Even then Maria had been hard and brazen, as though she weren't a young girl but some forest creature. The fear of that moment came back to me, and I moved on. My feet were heavy, but I walked without stumbling. The night light grew dimmer, but the brightness wasn't spoiled. The meadows spread out along the hilltops bathed in blue.

I knew something was amiss, but what it was exactly, I

couldn't say. It was as though my head was emptied. Now I felt a strong desire for a drink. For years no strong drink had passed my lips. What the women drank in prison was worse than sewage. I remembered that I had promised Benjamin that I wouldn't drink, but now I knew that I wouldn't be able to keep that promise. If a peasant came and offered me a drink, I'd grab it.

While I was standing there, given over to my desire, the heavens opened and a light from on high covered the blue meadows with a mighty splendor. I covered my face and knelt down.

"Katerina." I heard a voice.

"Your servant, my Lord," I answered immediately.

"Remove your shoes from your feet, because you are standing on a holy place."

I took off my shoes and sat, closing my eyes. For a long time I was withdrawn into myself, but the voice didn't speak to me again.

Later, when I raised my face, I saw ruins looming up before me, actually one ruin and two walls remaining from a building that had collapsed. The empty windows were full of light.

"What must I do, O Lord," I said, and I didn't know what I was saying.

The heavens did not open again, but the light was strong and my attention great. When I drew near the ruin, I saw with my own eyes that I hadn't been wrong. It was a Jewish ruin. There were still signs of a mezuzah on the doorpost. Everything, every shelf and hook, had been pulled from the walls, and what hadn't been ripped away by human hands had been tattered by the winds.

"I consecrate you as a temple," I said, and stepped inside. The light inside was sharper than outside. I put out my hands and wanted to call out, God in heaven, for I immediately saw that the dreadful rash had left my hands and they were as they had been, the fingers short and the thumb thick.

31

IN THE OPEN FIELDS there are no secrets. The peasant woman who happened upon me had spread the rumor, and the rumor had taken flight. Now peasants were standing on the hilltops and pointing at me: "There she is, the monster." Fierce was my desire to pluck off a branch and thrash them. My hands shook and I felt the power in them. Yet my legs were not what they used to be, now heavy and swollen. Still, I didn't hold my tongue but shouted, "Curs, you've slaughtered the priests and fouled the altar, and now God no longer dwells in this place."

That very night, I cushioned the floor of the temple with straw. Amazingly, that little bit of straw changed the look of the ruin, and I sat for hours and recited psalms. That chant exalted my senses, and afterward I could see only visions of light.

In the midst of this, summer ended. The fields turned brown and low clouds descended from above and spread over the fields. Suddenly, I saw the Jews of the autumn. The autumn Jews were lonely people, with long suitcases in their hands. They used to make their way by foot. The autumn Jews were mostly tall and you could find them leaning on a tree, next to a well, and sometimes at the edge of the village, sitting and observing. Children were afraid of them for some reason, and the adults would drive them away, the way you drive off an unfamiliar horse.

I spent most of the day in the ruin. Sometimes I felt that my distant years were close by, and I heard my mother's voice: "Where are you? Why don't you take the cattle out to pasture? It's late." Sometimes I heard nothing, I just saw: my mother in the dairy and my father next to the fence, swigging from the bottle. A cold and dissolute smile spread on his face, and not far from him were his two bastards, the way they had appeared once, cramped together on a little wagon, convicts on their way back to prison after a day's work.

Now the autumn was growing clearer, and I knew that there were no more Jews left in the world, and only within me had they found refuge for a moment. That knowledge filled me with sudden fear, and I went out. On the path above me rolled a wagon full of hay. The moment they noticed me, the peasants raised their arms and called out, "There she is, the monster." My hands were full of strength again, and I raised my voice and shouted, "Wicked curs. There were ancient priests among you, preserving the faith, and they colored this heaven with their holidays, merchants who bore precious fragrances in their suitcases. Those creatures, the tortured descendants of Jesus, wandered about here and reminded everyone that there is a life of truth. We hated them—there was no end to our hatred. We used to steal from them whenever we had an opportunity. We bit them and struck them. How we loved to batter them. And in the winter, we would go and hunt them. That's how it was, year after year. There was no end to our hatred. Now we have murdered them. We have murdered them completely, but you should know that no one in the village can say his hands didn't spill that blood."

For many hours I would wander along the streams. When it rained I would take shelter in the ruins. They were Jewish houses from which everything had been sundered. But to me those ruins were like temples. I knew every corner. Sometimes I would find a candlestick or a goblet, sacramental objects, and they would bring to mind the memory of the holidays, Passover and Shavuot.

Thus I walked from ruin to ruin. The nakedness was laid bare down to the marrow. But just there, among those straight-standing remains, the Jews were revealed to me as they never had been: hidden servants of God.

Only here did I dare ask to join that hidden tribe. Accept me, I asked. I didn't know whether I deserved that grace. I had no one in the world, only you. I wasn't asking for any special favor, neither here nor in the world of truth, just to be close to you. Ever since I met you for the first time, I have loved you. I love you the way you are. None of your manners disturb me, none of your movements. I love your movements as they are, without any change. If it were given to me to be among you, I would be. I can cook, sew, clean the yard, bring supplies from the market. I'm not so young anymore, but I can do all that work. You know me.

The cold days came, and I wept a lot. Boys stood on the hilltops and shouted, "There she is, the monster!" My desire was fierce to chase them, but I knew that my legs wouldn't carry me.

One evening, while I was still sitting and reciting psalms, I saw a young man sneaking into my door. I didn't hesitate, and with a sweep of my hand I caught him and told him, "What's the matter with you, you wicked thing." His face was small, like a shepherd's. Innocence was spread on his lips.

"I'm not guilty." He fluttered in my hands.

"Why did you shout 'monster?' "

"Everybody was shouting."

"From now on I'd better not hear that word," I said, and I threw him out. He stood for a moment, surprised he had escaped with such a light punishment. That week the fierce autumn winds came.

32

I FOUND SOME PAPER and a pencil, and I'm sitting and writing words to brighten my darkness. I write *shabbis* and again I write *shabbis*, and, marvelously, that single word has the power to evoke not only silence but also a melody. Since there are no longer any Jews left in the world, I make the Sabbath for myself every week. I drive away all evil thoughts within me and proclaim a Sabbath for the Lord, and for a whole day I wrap myself in it as in a cloak.

At the close of the Sabbath, to my surprise, I feel a thin sadness rise within me, and I know that the Sabbath queen, under whose wings I have hidden for a moment, is about to leave. The parting is hard for me, and I go out and watch the skies as they change, and the tender light is gradually swallowed up by the darkness.

Now I write down *shvues*, and immediately the scent of green plants and dairy products rises in my nose. On Shavuot, the house doors are open and warm air flows in. On Shavuot, the Torah was given from heaven, and Rosa wears a flowered dress, which she wears only on Shavuot.

Now I write *tishebov*. That was the gloomiest day of all. People fled from each other as though the angel of death were pursuing them. Benjamin wouldn't speak with anyone, his face was sealed, and Rosa curled up on the floor and read the dirges out loud. This is a destruction without end, a fault that cannot be mended; only the Messiah will come and repair it. And now I write down: *rosheshone* and *yonkiper* and *sukes* and *khanike* and *purim* and *tubishvas* and *peysekh* and on and on. I write and I compress the many lights together into words, so that the words will slow in my memory. I am afraid of the darkness. Now there are no more Jews left in the world, but a little of them is buried in my memory, and I am afraid that that little bit will be lost. My memory is weakening, and so I continue to write: *treyf, tume, orel*, Sabbath candles, Yom Kippur candles, *nile, kharoyses, tkin-khatsos, slikhes, shabesnakhmu, sude-hamafsekes*. I'm writing the words down in big letters, compressing a great deal of life into this envelope of words, because I am afraid of my memory. Here in this green desert a person can easily lose his memory. All the years I fought against oblivion, and now I feel I can no longer overcome it, and so I keep on writing.

At night the boys would come back from the school they called *hayder*. They carried little lanterns in their hands, and on the white snow they looked like two angels. Presently, I would take off their coats, and away they flew. Their father used to ask them a question about the Bible, and I couldn't understand a word. "What does Rashi say?" asked the father, and Abraham would give a long and apparently clear answer, and the father was pleased, but he didn't reveal his contentment easily.

Later I would hear the boys reciting the *Shema* before bedtime. That prayer brought a kind of new light to the house. In those years, may God forgive me, I didn't see the light around me. My body was in a turmoil, and I was immersed within myself with no way out. Now everything is far away and forgotten. The green lushness here is hard and thick, and so as not to slide into the abyss of emptiness, I write down: *simhistoyre, hakafis* little flags, with red apples on the end of the poles. Around me tall dogs bark, but the children wave their flags and proclaim: "There are no dogs, no wolves."

"Come, children, the time has come to return home." I hear Rosa's voice. It's hard to take the children away from the celebration, but Rosa draws them away, scolding them, and cuffing Abraham in the face. Now I'm not sure whether it really happened that way and if the dogs really barked or whether that was Simhat Torah or the day before Rosa was murdered. Rosa had strong hands, and she would hit the children hard. I am very sorry that she hit the children on the night before she was killed. One doesn't forget blows; they are sealed in our flesh.

After Benjamin's murder, I felt the trembling in my fingers for the first time. There had always been a kind of tremor in my fingers, but then I understood for the first time it was a tremor that had strength. After Benjamin was murdered, I told Rosa, "We ought to kill the murderer." Rosa heard my words but didn't respond, and I too was afraid to speak. When Rosa was murdered, I considered going out to the villages and looking for the killer. Now there are no more victims in the world, only murderers. Now I close my eyes and rest my head against the wall.

I envision the candles for Yom Kippur. Rosa used to make the candles for Yom Kippur with her own hands. She used to buy the beeswax from the mountain Jews. She would prepare everything with great care and quietly. What a simple life, what a full life. Only innocent people are not afraid of killers. Anyone born in a village knows that killers lurk in every den. More than once I wanted to shout, flee this evil place. But in my heart I knew that the people wouldn't listen to me. I had the senses of a peasant, and I knew that a killer would spare neither women nor children. I should have said it, I should have shouted, I should have taken them to a village and shown them how the killers act. I, may God forgive me, didn't know what to say or how to say it. Indeed my hands trembled, but I didn't know what they were telling me.

33

AFTER EASTER, as I mentioned, I returned to my native village and to my father's farm, small and dilapidated, with no building left intact except this hut where I'm living. But it has one single window, open wide, and it allows in the breadth of the world. My eyes, in truth, have grown weaker, but the desire to see still throbs within them. At noon, when the light is most powerful, open space expands before me as far as the banks of the Prut, whose water is blue this season, vibrant with splendor.

I left this place behind more than sixty years ago—to be precise, sixty-three years ago—but it hasn't changed much. The vegetation, that green eternity which envelops these hills, stands tall. If my eyes do not deceive me, it's even greener. A few trees from my distant childhood still stand straight and sprout leaves, not to mention that enchanting, wavelike movement of these hills. Everything is in its place, except for the people. They've all left and gone away.

In the early morning hours, I must remove the heavy veils

that obscure the many years and examine them, with silent observation, face to face, as they say in Scripture.

The summer nights in this season are long and splendid, and not only are the oaks reflected in the lake, but the simple reeds also draw vigor from that clear water. I always loved that modest lake, but I especially loved it during the brilliant summer nights, when the line between heaven and earth is erased and the whole cosmos is suffused with heavenly light. The years in a foreign land distanced me from these marvels, and they were obliterated from my memory, but not, apparently, from my heart. Now I know that light is what drew me back. Such purity, oh Lord! Sometimes I wish to stretch out my hand and touch the breezes that meet me on my way, because in this season they are soft as silk.

It's hard to sleep on these brilliant summer nights. Sometimes it seems to me that it's a sin to sleep in this brilliance. I understand now what it says in the Holy Scriptures: "He who stretches out the heaven like a thin curtain." The word *curtain* always sounded strange and distant. Now I can see the thin curtain.

Walking is very hard for me. Without the broad window, which is open wide, without it taking me out and bringing me in, I would be locked up here like in prison, but this opening, by its grace, brings me out easily, and I wander over the meadows as in my youth. Late at night, when the light dims on the horizon, I return to my cage, my hunger sated and my thirst slaked, and I shut my eyes. When I close my eyes I encounter other faces, faces I haven't seen before.

On Sundays I pull myself together and go down to the chapel. The distance from my hut to the chapel isn't great, a quarter of an hour's walk. In my youth I used to cover the distance in a single bound. Then all my life was a single puff of breeze, but today, though every step is painful, that walk is still very important to me. These stones awaken my memory, especially the memory from before memory, and I see not only my departed mother but everyone who ever passed over these paths, knelt, wept, and prayed. For some reason it now seems they all used to wear fur coats. Maybe because of a nameless peasant, who came here secretly, prayed, and afterward took his life with his own hand. His shouts pierced my temples.

The chapel building is old and rickety yet lovely in its simplicity. The wooden buttresses that my father installed still protect it. My father wasn't scrupulous about keeping our religion, but he saw it as his duty not to neglect this small sanctuary. I remember, as though in a twilight, the beams he carried on his shoulders, thick staves, and the way he pounded them into the earth with a huge wooden mallet. My father seemed like a giant to me then, and his work was the work of giants. Those beams, though they've rotted, are still rooted in their place. Inanimate objects live a long life, only man is snatched away untimely.

Whoever thought I would come back here? I had erased this first bosom from my memory like an animal, but a person's memory is stronger than he is. What the will doesn't do is done by necessity, and necessity ultimately becomes will. I'm not sorry I returned. Apparently, it was ordained.

I sit on the low bench in the chapel for an hour or two. The silence here is massive, perhaps because of the valley that surrounds the place. As a girl I used to run after cows and goats on these trails. How blind and marvelous my life was then. I was like one of the animals I drove, strong like them and just as mute. Of those years no outward trace remains, just me, the years crammed into me, and my old age. Old age brings a person closer to himself and to the dead. The beloved dead bring us close to God.

In this valley I heard a voice from on high for the first time—actually, it was in the lowest slopes of this valley, where it opens up and flows into a broad plain. I remember the voice with great clarity. I was seven, and suddenly I heard a voice, not my mother's or father's, and the voice said to me, "Don't be afraid, my daughter. You shall find the lost cow." It was an assured voice, and so calm that it instantly removed the fear from my heart. I sat frozen and watched. The darkness grew thicker. There was no sound, and suddenly the cow emerged from the darkness and came up to me. Ever since then, when I hear the word *salvation*, I see that brown cow I had lost and who came back. That voice addressed me only once, never again. I never told anyone about it. I kept that secret hidden in my heart, and I rejoiced in it. In those years I was afraid of every shadow. In truth, I was prey to fear for many years and only free of it when I reached an advanced age. If I had prayed, prayer would have taught me not to be afraid. But my fate decreed otherwise, if I may say. The lesson came to me many years too late, immersed in many bitter experiences.

In my youth, I had no desire either for prayer or for the Holy Scriptures. The words of prayers that I intoned were not my own. I went to church because my mother forced me. At the age of twelve, I had visions of obscenities in the middle of prayers, which greatly darkened my spirit. Every

Sunday I used to pretend to be sick, and as much as my mother hit me, nothing did any good. I was as afraid of church as I was of the village doctor.

Nevertheless, thank God, I didn't cut myself off from the wellsprings of faith. There were moments in my life when I forgot myself, when I sank into filth, when I lost the image of God, but even then I would fall to my knees and pray. Remember, God, those few moments, because my sins were many, and only Thou, with Thy great mercy, know the soul of Thy handmaiden.

Now, as the proverb says, the water has flowed back into the river, the circle is closed, and I have returned here. Too bad the dead are forbidden to speak. They'd have something to say, I'm sure. But the days are full and splendid, and I wander at great length. As long as the window is open and my eyes are awake, loneliness doesn't grieve my soul.

ABOUT THE TYPE

This book was set in Galliard, a typeface designed by
Matthew Carter for the Mergenthaler Linotype Company in 1978. Galliard is based on the sixteenth-
century typefaces of Robert Granjon, which gives it
classic lines yet interject a contemporary look.